COUNTERPLAY

COUNTERPLAY

Copyright © 2019 Ceara Nobles.

For information contact :
Ceara Nobles
https://www.cearanobles.com

Cover design by Germancreative © 2019 Ceara Nobles
Book Formatting by Derek Murphy @Creativindie

First Edition: 2019

10 9 8 7 6 5 4 3 2 1

COUNTERPLAY

An ESI Novel

CEARA NOBLES

Riverside
PRESS

ALSO BY

CEARA NOBLES

THE ESI SERIES

DUAL INNOCENCE

LEGACY EXPOSED

TRUTH REVEALED

SIGN UP FOR MY MONTHLY NEWSLETTER

TO RECEIVE SPECIAL OFFERS, GIVEAWAYS, DISCOUNTS, BONUS CONTENT, UPDATES FROM THE AUTHOR, INFO ON NEW RELEASES AND OTHER GREAT READS:

WWW.CEARANOBLES.COM/SUBSCRIBE

For my daughter Annabelle... You are my greatest adventure.

PROLOGUE

Five Years Ago...

ROMAN TAPPED THE BOTTOM of the magazine in his M4, ensuring it was firmly in place, and pulled the charging handle toward him. The sound echoed in the jungle around him, but surveillance had already determined that the area was clear.

He released a breath and checked his earpiece. The quiet static assured him it was working properly, even though his team was operating on radio silence.

"We're passing Alpha," a voice spoke into the radio. It was Jeffries, team lead. As usual, he was calm and collected despite the fact that they were about to engage in a firefight with one of the most dangerous drug lords in the world.

They were just outside the Golden Triangle, which meant a firefight here could bring several neighboring cartels down on them before they could make an escape.

But they had the opportunity to cut off the head of the snake, and the United States government wouldn't let that pass them by, no matter the risk.

Roman's intel from two years undercover had gotten them here, and many lives had been lost to find the location of Altez's compound. After today, Roman's cover would be compromised. He could never go back to the cartel again.

It was now or never.

Roman crept through the trees, using the shadows to blend into his surroundings as he approached the main building of the compound. His teammates were doing the same thing on the south, west, and north sides of the structure.

Altez was sure of his safety near the Golden Triangle. He didn't even have a wall surrounding his massive home. No cameras, towers, or guards aside from the two posted just outside his front door.

Roman crouched in a tall bush just outside the radius of light from the door and pulled his night-vision goggles down around his neck. He took aim at the guards and waited.

"Breach," Jeffries ordered over the radio.

Roman's first shot hit the left guard in the forehead. Thanks to the suppressor on the end of Roman's gun, the man dropped before his partner even knew what happened. Before the second guard could react, Roman took a second shot and dropped him too.

Although he couldn't hear accompanying gunfire, Roman knew his team was breaching the house from the other entry points.

"Front door is clear," Roman said. "I'm entering the building."

He kicked open the front door and swung his gun in a wide arc. A man popped out of a side door, assault rifle aimed at Roman, but Roman took him out before he could get off a shot.

One by one, his team cleared the rooms on the lower level. Altez was nowhere to be found, and they only ran into a handful of guards.

"Just passed Charlie," Jeffries said into the comms. "Clear the upper floor. I'll watch for stragglers."

Roman led the way upstairs, moving slow and precise. He could feel more than hear his teammates behind him. It was comforting that he had someone on his six, so he could focus on the area in front of him.

He kicked open the first door on the right. A high-pitched scream split the darkness and Roman ducked away from the light flooding in from the hallway. The loud bang of a gunshot echoed not even a second later, followed by a thud.

"Wilson is down," Martinez said into the comms.

Roman cursed silently and yanked his night-vision goggles back up over his eyes. In the green filter, he saw a woman standing in the corner of the bedroom, a gun shaking in front of her. He couldn't make out many details, but she was blonde and wearing a short nightgown. The covers on the bed were rumpled as if she'd just rolled out of them.

"Put the gun down," Roman yelled.

The woman turned and fired blindly in his direction.

He ducked and trained his gun on her again. "Ma'am, put the gun down or I will shoot you."

She shouted a stream of panicked Spanish, but she didn't lower the weapon.

Roman cursed. "Where is Altez? *¿Dónde está Altez?*"

"Roman. Report," Jeffries said in Roman's earpiece.

The woman shook her head. The barrel of the gun shook harder. She was crying now, shouting in broken Spanish. Roman had five years of Spanish under his belt, but he couldn't understand a word she was saying.

"Put the weapon down," he warned. "I don't want to shoot you."

"Holt. Report," Jeffries said again.

"There's a woman here with a gun," Martinez reported. "I'm pinned down in the hallway with Wilson. I can't get to him."

"I'm coming," Jeffries said. "Holt, don't move. Keep her occupied, but don't shoot her. She may know where Altez is."

Easier said than done.

"I don't want to hurt you," Roman said to the woman in Spanish. "Please, put the gun down."

She shook her head, sobbing, and backed up a few steps until her back hit the wall. Her gun was pointing in his general direction, but it was too dark for her to see him. Luckily, she was smart enough not to shoot blindly again.

Footsteps echoed in the hall.

Jeffries appeared in the doorway just as the woman swung her gun around. The barrel steadied, and she let out a breath as she readied to fire.

Roman shot her before she could pull the trigger. She dropped like a stone.

Jeffries rushed forward and kicked the gun away from her limp hands. Roman dropped to his knees next to her and felt his stomach keep falling.

Blood bloomed from a hole in her chest, right where her heart was.

She didn't have a pulse.

Jeffries cursed and lowered his gun, his expression grim. "That's Maria, Altez's wife."

Roman swallowed hard.

This was their only chance to catch him.

Roman had just killed an innocent woman, and Altez got away.

CHAPTER 1

Three weeks ago...

"SARAH ERICKSON!"

The blaring beauty of 80's rock turned tinny as Sarah's headphones were yanked off her ears. She jerked her head up from the medical textbook she'd been squinting at.

"What the?"

Ryan stood with his hands on his hips, camera swinging from the strap around his neck. "I've been calling you for ten minutes. Would it kill you to turn the music off?"

Sarah stuck her tongue out. "First you tell me to wear headphones because it's *interrupting your concentration*" - she emphasized the phrase with air quotes – "and now you're telling me to turn it off?"

"You can't even retain anything with music that loud."

"Says who?"

"I think your grades speak for themselves."

Sarah glared at Ryan, and he glared right back.

Then they both busted up laughing.

"What do you need?" Sarah asked when they had both calmed down. "I'm trying to get some studying in before my shift starts."

Ryan looked down at her EMT uniform. "Are you on ambulance duty tonight?"

"Yeah, until three a.m. Now, what do you want?"

Ryan made a face and raised his camera, snapping a picture of her before she could duck out of sight. Instead of grinning at her like he usually would, his expression stayed sober. "I'm going out for a while. Just wanted to let you know so you didn't freak out."

"Now?" Sarah touched the screen of her phone, squinting at the date. "But it's Tuesday."

"I know. You're going to have to eat Chinese without me." Ryan backed up a few steps, raising a hand. "I've got something important to do. I'll see you later."

"Wait," Sarah said, following him down the hallway and into the living room. "What's more important than Chinese food?"

Ryan pulled on his jacket, hesitated, and then disappeared into his bedroom. He emerged a moment later without his camera. He gave Sarah a kiss on the cheek as he passed, but his expression was already somewhere else.

"Loveyoubye," he said over his shoulder as he closed the front door behind him.

Sarah frowned at the closed door. "Loveyoubye," she murmured.

She took a few moments to ponder Ryan's strange attitude, but she had a test the next morning and only a limited amount of time before her shift started.

* * * * *

Ambulance duty was Sarah's favorite shift. She thrived on the challenge of each call, and she loved helping people.

That night was a quiet one. Between New York City's astronomical crime rate and the insane amount of people living in a small area, her team was usually pretty busy, but they only had one call during Sarah's shift – a car accident with only minor injuries.

Sarah sat with Jackson and Nora, her partner and driver respectively, and played cards during the downtime. She should have been studying, but her brain was fried. She'd rather be paid to play Texas Hold 'Em than study for her biology test.

It was almost 3 a.m. when the station's alert tone sounded in the speaker above their heads.

"So close," Jackson groaned, getting to his feet. He was an older guy, in his mid-forties. "I was looking forward to going to bed at a decent time tonight."

"Got one more in you?" Nora asked with a smile.

"Ugh, I guess so."

Sarah jumped to her feet and put her ear close to the speaker, listening as the dispatcher rattled off an address. "It's a mugging," she said. "Severe injury, possibly fatal."

Jackson rubbed his neck. "Why do you sound excited about that?"

Sarah grinned. "I love this job."

"Yeah, you love it a little too much."

Nora opened the door to the garage, keys jingling in

her hand. "Come on, let's do this. I'd like to get home at a decent time too."

The mugging had occurred in Chelsea. Back in the day, the neighborhood was known for its drug activity, but lately, the crime of choice was theft – larceny, muggings, bank robberies. Sarah had been to the area multiple times in her three years of EMS work.

By the time their ambulance arrived on the scene, it was already roped off and several police cars sat nearby with their lights flashing.

Sarah hopped out, Jackson right behind her, and hurried toward the crowd forming at the entrance to an alley. They parted for her like the Red Sea, and she ducked under the police tape.

A policeman waved her over to where the victim lay, another policeman administering CPR.

Sarah dropped to her knees next to the man, her eyes scanning his body for obvious injuries. A dark stain on his coat was already spreading.

"He's hardly breathing," the policeman next to her said, sounding out of breath. "I've been doing CPR but he needs a doctor. Now."

Sarah nodded and gestured for him to move. "We'll take care of him."

She opened the man's coat and lifted up his shirt, exposing the stab wound in his chest. It was just below his heart, but that didn't mean he was safe. There were plenty of other vital organs in that area that could be affected.

"Sir, I'm going to need you to –"

Sarah froze when she finally looked at the man's face.

"R-Ryan?"

Ryan's face was barely recognizable. His cheeks were swollen, his eyes nearly shut, and blood from his broken nose smeared his skin.

He tried to smile at her, but it looked more like a grimace. "I was hoping you'd come," he said softly.

"Ryan, what..." Sarah looked down at the wound on his chest, horror spreading through her like wildfire. "What happened? What are you doing in Chelsea?"

Ryan wheezed a breath, his eyes fluttering closed.

Jackson kneeled next to her. One glance at the damage and he called over his shoulder for Nora to bring the stretcher. "What are you doing?" he said impatiently. "We need to stop the bleeding."

"This is Ryan, my roommate."

For the first time in her career, she felt completely frozen.

Jackson spared her a pitying look. "Now isn't the time to freeze on me, Erickson. Help Nora with the stretcher. Move!"

Sarah stumbled to her feet and ran to the ambulance. She took one end of the stretcher and they hurried it back to Ryan's side. Jackson was already taping gauze over the wound, muttering soothing words.

Ryan appeared to be unconscious. Sarah dropped to her knees and put a finger to the pulse on his neck. It was weak, barely there at all.

"Ryan," she said urgently. "Ryan, you need to wake up. We're going to help you, but you need to wake up."

Ryan didn't move.

"CPR, Erickson, let's go," Jackson snapped.

Sarah bit back a sob and placed her hands over Ryan's chest. She counted the compressions aloud, anything to keep herself from completely losing it.

"We're losing him," Jackson said. "Nora, grab the defib kit."

Sarah put her mouth over his. His chest rose with the force of her air. "Come on, Ryan," she muttered.

"I think his lung is punctured," Jackson said. "His skin is turning blue. He's not getting enough oxygen."

Ryan's eyelids fluttered open. He focused on her, and his lips twitched in another smile. "Sorry," he said softly.

"Shh," Sarah said. "You're going to be fine. Hang in there, okay?"

His eyes closed again.

Sarah looked up at Jackson. The grim expression on his face told her everything she needed to know.

"No. He's going to be fine, right?"

Jackson placed a silent hand on her shoulder.

Sarah shook it off, turning back to Ryan. She grabbed his hand and squeezed it tight. "Ryan, can you hear me?"

No answer.

She dropped his hand and started doing compressions again. She counted to thirty, gave him three breaths, and started all over again.

"Sarah," Jackson said from beside her, voice gentle.

Sarah shook her head and continued her compressions. She wouldn't give up on him. She'd seen people survive worse.

He was a fighter. He could fight through it.

"Sarah, he's gone, sweetheart."

Sarah opened her eyes, her hands slowing on Ryan's chest. With shaking fingers, she touched his neck.

No pulse.

Nora stepped up next to them, the defib kit in her hands. Jackson shook his head at her, then took Sarah's arm and pulled her to her feet.

He led her back to the ambulance and sat her down on the edge.

Sarah watched as he covered Ryan's body with a black sheet. He conversed with the head policeman, probably ordering a coroner to the scene.

She barely registered when her phone rang. With numb fingers, she pulled it out of her pocket.

"Hello?" Her voice sounded hollow, even to her.

"Sarah." It was Owen, her twin brother. His voice sounded worse than she felt. "Sorry to call you this late, but..."

Sarah swallowed hard. "What's wrong?"

"It's time to come home." A long pause. "It's Dad."

CHAPTER 2

DEATH CAME FOR EVERYONE EVENTUALLY, but it really sucked to be the one left behind.

Sarah was becoming too familiar with that role. Death had been following her around like a jealous ex-boyfriend for months now. She'd feel better if she was the target, but apparently she was the "lucky" one who stuck around to pick up the pieces after her loved ones were gone.

She stood in the middle of her apartment living room, hands on hips. Towering stacks of boxes rendered the room unrecognizable, and she was only halfway done.

How was she supposed to box all of this up by herself? Half of this stuff wasn't even hers. Who was she to decide what went to charity and what went to the landfill?

With a sigh, she shimmied a box from a nearby pile and sidestepped into an empty space to continue the grueling job.

The silence got to her faster than she expected. Even

three weeks after Ryan's death, she still wasn't used to it. She found herself straining to hear his muttering as he studied, or the soft "snick" of his camera as he took pictures of the skyline from their living room window.

"Eye of the Tiger" sounded from Sarah's back pocket.

Grateful for the distraction, she pulled out her phone.

"Hi, honey." Her mother's cheerful voice was a stark contrast to the gloomy pall over the apartment. "How's the packing going?"

Sarah pasted on a smile. Mary could smell a frown even from the other side of the country, and Sarah was *not* ready to explain why she was standing here fighting tears. "Great," she lied. "Almost done. I shouldn't be too much longer."

"Oh, good. When will you be home? These disaster cleanup people are destroying the house. I need someone to talk some sense into them, and Owen is working. I haven't seen him in days. These people won't listen to a word I say."

Sarah sighed. "Mom, their job is to clean all the water out of the basement and estimate the damages. Most of the stuff down there is ruined now anyway. Just let them do their jobs."

"I know, but your father's study..." Mary's voice wobbled. "He wouldn't like the mess."

Sarah swallowed hard. Another victim of her cursed luck -- as if she needed to be reminded that he was gone. "I know. My flight leaves tonight. I'll be home in the morning. For now, just... let them do their thing. We'll clean everything up when they're done."

Mary's dramatic sigh echoed in Sarah's ear. "All right. Call me when you get to the airport. Owen or I will come pick you up. I love you."

"Love you too." Sarah hung up, rubbing the bridge of her nose. An ache was starting right behind her eyes. If she didn't get this packing over with quickly, it would turn into a full migraine and then she would be useless. She looked around the apartment and then down to the empty box in her other hand. "Well," she said to the silence. "Let's get this over with."

Packing her bedroom wasn't hard. She started there first - one pile to take home, and another pile to donate. It was a much easier decision to make with her own possessions. One by one, the pieces of her life in New York filled the donation pile. Her medical textbooks. Her EMT uniform, still stained with Ryan's blood.

New York just wasn't her reality anymore.

Sarah glanced across the hall to Ryan's closed bedroom door.

The reality was, her best friend was dead. And she couldn't live in New York without him.

All too soon, her bedroom was finished, and she was forced to move to Ryan's room. She opened the door and his smell assaulted her; coffee and woodsy aftershave. Her stomach twisted itself in knots as her gaze wandered the room, from his bed with its still-rumpled sheets to the mess of papers and books scattered across his desk.

If she didn't know better, she'd think he'd only left the room moments before. That he'd merely taken a break from studying for his next exam. Any moment he'd yell across the hall that she'd better be studying too or she'd fail another test.

Sarah's eyes stung. She bit her lip to keep the tears from falling. Now wasn't the time for a breakdown. She had too much to do.

The creak of her front door's hinge sounded loud in the silent apartment.

Sarah froze, one hand resting on Ryan's stack of textbooks.

She always locked the front door. Had she been so preoccupied that she forgot?

No, she distinctly remembered turning the deadbolt.

Sarah reached under her shirt, then remembered that her pistol was sitting in the nightstand back at Chance's house.

No matter. She was trained in hand-to-hand combat, courtesy of her ex-military brothers. If her visitor turned out to be unfriendly, she could take care of herself.

A loud clatter sounded as a tower of boxes fell over in the living room, followed by a muttered curse.

Whoever it was, they weren't bothering to be quiet.

Sarah slipped out of Ryan's room, grabbing the wooden baseball bat he kept behind his door in case of emergencies.

"David, I'll be right there," she called.

Maybe it was a burglar and he'd be smart enough to run away.

No further sound came from the living room.

Swallowing hard, Sarah came down the hall, swinging the baseball bat casually in front of her.

A Hispanic man stood in the middle of her living room, staring back at her. A stack of boxes was collapsed at his feet, spewing a bunch of Ryan's things.

"Oh, hi," she said brightly. "I'm sorry, who are you?"

The man hesitated a moment. His eyes went from her face to the baseball bat swinging at her waist. "I'm Jose," he said slowly. "I was one of Ryan's friends. The door was open."

Bull.

She knew all of Ryan's friends, and she'd locked that door.

Sarah maintained her distance, but kept the friendly expression on her face. "Ah, I see. As Ryan's friend, I'm sure you heard what happened."

"Yeah, I'm sorry. I worked with him and I just came by to see if I could get my SD card."

Sarah's eyes narrowed. "SD card?"

"He was taking some pictures for me and I gave him my SD card. I was hoping to get it back, now that... you know." Jose had the grace to look abashed, but his body language was too tense to pull it off.

Sarah pulled out her phone. "Well, he took his camera with him that night, so the police have it. I know the sergeant that worked on his case, though, so let me call him and-"

"No," Jose said hastily, raising his hands. "That's okay. I'll just... buy a new SD card."

"Good idea." Sarah smiled sweetly. "You know where the door is."

Jose looked at her for a moment longer.

Sarah tightened her grip on the bat, dialed 911 on the phone in her left hand, and readied herself for a fight.

Then he nodded and left the apartment without another word.

Sarah rushed to the door and flipped the deadbolt, securing the chain too for good measure. She looked through the peephole, but the hallway appeared to be empty.

Goosebumps broke out over her skin.

She'd just avoided a potentially dangerous situation.

Why the hell had she left her gun in La Conner?

She reached into a nearby box and grabbed a bottle of pepper spray. It didn't have the stopping power of a .38 round, but it would do in a pinch.

She shoved it into her pocket and returned to Ryan's room to finish packing.

It took her a few minutes to calm down after her near-danger experience. She sat for a few minutes on Ryan's bed, running her hands over the rumpled sheets.

Finally, she slid off the mattress and to the floor.

Jose had been looking for an SD card. Sarah hadn't been completely honest with him; Ryan *didn't* take his camera with him that night.

As a matter of fact, she distinctly remembered him returning to the bedroom to leave it here. It was out of character for him; he went everywhere with that camera.

She looked around. It wasn't sitting on his desk or his bed. His closet was far too messy for him to put it in there.

Where else would he hide it?

She reached under Ryan's bed and her fingers wrapped

around his Nikon. She pulled it out and smiled.

On her first day at NYU - wow, was that six years ago already? - he took a picture of her during orientation. He struck up a conversation with her and they realized they were both aspiring med students. They'd been inseparable ever since.

Sarah turned the camera over in her hands, smiling at the scratches and dings. Ryan always told her that life was short, and the only way to keep a moment forever was to document it. The evidence of that belief was taped on every inch of his bedroom walls in the form of hundreds of photos.

Pictures of Sarah, their classes, NYU campus, the coffee shop where Ryan worked in his spare time. They provided a glimpse into Ryan's life, but he was so much more than that.

Sarah could tell the story behind every picture; she'd been there for most of them.

Sarah popped open the SD card slot and sure enough, there was a blue piece of plastic lodged inside.

Was this the SD card Jose was looking for?

What could be so important that he would break into a dead man's apartment to find it?

Sarah closed the slot and turned on the camera. She pressed the review button, but the tiny screen went black. White letters flashed across the screen.

File Corrupted.

Well, if she ever saw Jose again, she'd have to break the bad news to him.

Not that she ever would see his face again. She was

leaving New York tonight and never coming back.

Swallowing hard, she placed Ryan's camera in her suitcase and continued packing. Ryan's photos remained on his bedroom walls; she couldn't bear to take them down.

By the time she was almost finished, Sarah was exhausted. Her watch told her she needed to leave for the airport soon or she'd miss her flight. She pulled open the top drawer of Ryan's nightstand and grabbed the last stack of papers. Her knuckles rapped against the back of the drawer and she paused.

It sounded... hollow.

She tossed the papers into the open box beside her and knelt to peer into the drawer. She knocked on the side, the bottom, and then the back.

Yep, definitely hollow.

"What the...?" she muttered.

She ran her fingers across the seam. Her nails snagged on a small indent in the corner. If she wasn't looking for it, she would've thought it was a natural dip in the wood. She used her fingernail to tug on the indent.

The back of the drawer came away.

A false back.

Heart pounding, Sarah dropped it onto the floor and stuck her hand back into the shadowed recess of the drawer. Her fingers brushed against something small and she pulled it out.

A cell phone.

Not just any cell phone, but an old flip phone that looked like it was from the early 2000s. In fact, she'd had a similar phone in junior high. Sarah flipped it open and hit the power button. The screen blinked on, but it needed a pin to unlock it. She tried a few of the ones she knew Ryan used - his birthday, his ATM pin, his school ID number.

None of them worked.

Sarah frowned at the screen, growing more confused by the second.

First, the weird guy looking for an SD card... and now this.

Ryan had always been a technology guy. He spent all of his extra money on staying up-to-date with the latest gadgets. He wouldn't be caught dead with anything that was more than a year old.

So why would he keep this old thing hidden in a secret compartment in his bedroom?

Too many things didn't make sense.

Had Ryan gotten involved in something he shouldn't have?

She thought back to the past few months. Strange absences, phone calls he didn't want her to overhear, sudden secrecy.

Oh God, why hadn't she seen the signs?

Did that mean... his death wasn't a mugging?

Loud banging sounded from the front of the apartment.

Sarah jumped to her feet, heart pounding. Was Jose back? This time, he probably wouldn't leave so easily.

She shoved the flip phone into her back pocket and headed for the living room.

Halfway across the living room, she pulled out her pepper spray and rested her finger on the button.

It may not stop him, but it would immobilize him long enough for her to kick him in the balls and make a run for it.

She put her eye to the peephole.

It wasn't Jose.

"Are you freaking kidding me?" She threw open the door, eyes narrowed at the man standing in her hallway. "Roman."

He stood easily, hands in the pockets of his jeans. His dark brown eyes swept over her, landing on the pepper spray in her hand, and as usual, his expression was impossible to read. The wicked scar that stretched from the top of his left eyebrow to just below his eye combined with his slightly crooked nose made him look permanently angry.

Despite the fact that her brothers assured her he was a teddy bear, he looked like the type of guy you pepper sprayed and then ran away.

"Pepper spray?" he inquired.

"What?" Had she spoken her thoughts aloud?

He gestured at the can in her hand.

"Oh. Don't ask." Sarah threw the can into a nearby box. "Did my brothers send you here to babysit me? That's low, even for them. Besides, you're too late. I'm just heading to the airport."

He raised his eyebrows at her. "What are you doing here?"

"Excuse me? I should be asking you the same thing. This is my apartment."

Roman stepped into the living room - without asking for permission - and closed the door behind him. He locked the doorknob and the deadbolt before turning to face her.

Sarah watched his eyes travel from one pile of boxes to another, and finally back to her.

"What are you doing?" he asked.

She gestured to the room. "Packing. Obviously."

"How do you know Ryan?"

Wait, what?

Sarah took a step back so he wasn't towering over her and crossed her arms over her chest. Nobody in her family knew about Ryan. Had her brothers been keeping closer tabs on her than she'd thought? "How do *you* know Ryan? What are you even doing here?"

Roman stepped further into the room, turning away from her. "He was my brother."

Had she fallen and bumped her head? Was this the Twilight Zone? "Ryan doesn't have a brother."

"He does. I'm three years older."

"Hold the phone. I've known him for six years and he's never mentioned a brother."

"He wouldn't have. We're not close."

Sarah plopped down on the couch. She grabbed the end of her ponytail and twirled it in her fingers, as if it would help her wrap her brain around this. She knew Ryan. He never would have kept something like this from her.

But apparently, he associated with creepy guys like Jose and kept an old cell phone in a hidden compartment in his nightstand. How well did she really know him?

Sarah cleared her throat. "Do you... have you heard what happened?"

Roman shook his head. He seemed to be taking this coincidence a lot better than she was. "Not much. Can you tell me?"

She swallowed hard. That night was kind of a blur, but she did remember the blood. And begging him not to die even as she watched the light fade from his eyes. She would see that memory in her nightmares for the rest of her life. "It was a mugging," she said quietly. "About three weeks ago."

Roman placed a hand on one of the boxes and stared hard at it. "That's what I heard."

Sarah blinked the moisture from her eyes and cleared her throat. She made a show of glancing at her watch, then stood. "Listen, I gotta go. I know you work with my brothers, but please don't say anything about this. I haven't told my family."

Roman pinned her with a stare. "Why not?"

She'd been wondering the same thing herself. "I just... don't want to deal with them about it. With Dad's death and Bellamy's whole thing, they've got enough on their plates right now."

Ryan's hidden cell phone felt like it was burning a hole in her back pocket. Surely she could voice her fears to Roman, right? He was Ryan's brother.

"Besides, I have this weird feeling. I don't think Ryan's death was an accident."

Roman's back straightened and his eyebrows knitted together. The scar through his left eye distorted with the movement, turning white against his dark skin. "What makes you say it wasn't an accident?"

"Just a feeling, I guess. He's been acting weird for the past few months. And then I had this stranger show up here-"

"He was a weird guy. Let it go."

Sarah frowned at the rough edge in his voice. "Excuse me?"

Roman turned away from her, but his voice was low and hard. "You might think you knew Ryan, but you didn't. He went through weird stages all the time where he'd run off and disappear for no reason. He liked his secrecy. It's best if you go home to your family and get on with your life. There's no reason to chase ghosts."

She blinked at him in disbelief. "I've been living with Ryan for the past six years. He didn't even mention you. So which of us knows him better, do you think?"

"Ryan was killed in a random act of violence. I don't need his little friend poking around and sticking her nose where it doesn't belong. So I'm telling you to butt out and go back home to your family." He glanced at his watch. "You're going to miss your flight if you don't hurry."

Sarah's jaw dropped. She was too outraged to even form a response.

This guy might be Ryan's brother, but clearly he didn't care about Ryan at all.

She stomped to her bedroom and grabbed her suitcase. At the moment, she couldn't care less about finishing the last of her packing. Her landlord could deal with it; she was already going to lose her deposit.

Without a word to Roman, who was still standing where she'd left him, she stormed out of the apartment and slammed the door behind her.

* * * * *

Roman stood in his brother's apartment, at a loss.

Out of the millions of people in New York...

Of course Ryan's roommate had to be Sarah Erickson.

His boss's little sister.

The girl he had stupidly kissed a week ago, and who hadn't left his thoughts since.

Roman ran a hand through his hair, observing the stacks of boxes around him.

Was this Sarah's idea of cleaning up?

Most of their stuff was still here.

He looked through a few of the open boxes but didn't find anything interesting.

As if the answers to his questions would be here.

Ryan wasn't the type to leave important information lying around.

Roman wandered down the hallway, opening doors as he went. Bathroom. Laundry room.

Ooh, Sarah's bedroom.

The white comforter and faintly perfume scent gave it away, though most of the personal items were gone.

Roman was tempted to look through the three boxes stacked on the bed, but he shook himself. He had more important things to do.

He crossed the hall to Ryan's bedroom. The walls were lined with photos. Sarah hadn't taken them down.

He paused to observe a few of them. Sarah was the focus of many; brushing her teeth, studying, walking down the street.

He hadn't spoken to Ryan in years, but it was clear he had strong feelings for Sarah.

And she him, apparently.

That pissed him off.

If she had feelings for Ryan, why did she let Roman kiss her?

Not that he had paused to ask for permission... but she had definitely kissed him back.

Roman thumbed through some papers, looked through some boxes, but he didn't find anything out of the ordinary.

A few minutes later, his phone rang.

It was Jeffries, his old friend and former team lead.

"Roman, I've got some news for you."

"What is it?"

"They ruled Ryan's death as a random mugging, but they found his wallet in a dumpster a few blocks away. The cash and credit cards were still inside."

Roman's gut tightened. "It wasn't a mugging."

"No."

Roman released a breath. "It has to be Altez. He found Ryan somehow, and he killed him in retaliation."

"I don't know." Jeffries paused. "Maybe. I've been keeping tabs on the chatter and I haven't seen anything out of the ordinary, but Altez has been known to operate under the radar."

"I'm going to the coroner's office. They haven't released Ryan's body yet, so I'm going to see if I can find something."

"You sure that's a good idea? His body isn't going to look great after this long on ice."

Just the thought of it made Roman queasy. "I have to. It might be the only lead we have."

But as usual, he wasn't so lucky.

By the time he arrived at the coroner's office, the tech informed him that Ryan's body had been incinerated that morning.

Roman was right back to where he started.

His little brother was dead, and Roman knew who killed him.

But he couldn't prove it.

* * * * *

The flight back to Seattle was uneventful, but Sarah was still irate when she got off the plane the next morning.

How could Roman talk like that? It was so opposite of the man she'd kind of worked with over the past two weeks. The man who'd kissed her in the hallway at ESI just a week before.

His brother, her *best friend*, was dead. If there was any chance of foul play, didn't Roman want to know the truth?

Ryan's secret phone was in her purse. It felt like a fifty-pound weight with every step she took.

She needed to know what was on it.

If Ryan had gotten involved in something, she needed to find the person responsible for his death.

Maybe justice wouldn't bring him back, but it would certainly help Sarah sleep at night.

True to her word, Sarah's mother had arranged for Owen to pick her up. When she entered the parking garage, she found him waiting patiently, leaning against the door of his SUV. He pushed off with a smile and pulled her into a one-armed hug.

Sarah smiled up at him. Even though they were twins, they didn't look very much alike. They shared the same blond hair and green eyes, but that's where the resemblance ended. Owen had their father's looks; tall and athletic, with hair that always looked as if he'd just slept on it.

It was a running joke in the family. Owen didn't actually get much sleep. He was a night owl and often spent all night on his computer, so no one understood how he had an eternal bedhead.

"How was your flight?" Owen asked. He took her bag from her and threw it in the back seat.

"Fine." She climbed into the front and leaned her head back against the seat. She'd hoped to get some sleep on the plane, but instead she'd spent the whole time fuming about Roman and thinking herself in circles about Ryan.

Owen started the engine and pulled out of the parking garage. "Apartment all packed?"

"Yep."

Owen didn't say anything else; he didn't need to. They lapsed into a comfortable silence on the hour-and-a-half drive home to La Conner. Sarah stared out the window, allowing her eyes to drift closed. If either of her other brothers had picked her up, she would've been subject to interrogation the whole way home.

Why was she moving home? What about medical school? Where would she live? How long did she plan to stay?

Sarah didn't have any of those answers, so she was grateful that Owen had been the one to pick her up. He knew her better than anyone else, and he probably sensed she needed the silence.

Good thing, too, because she found herself drifting off to sleep.

She woke up when they hit the gravel drive that led to her parents' house.

Well, it was just her mom's house now. She'd never get used to calling it that, no matter how long her father's body rested in the cemetery.

The house came into view when they rounded the corner, its lines more familiar to her than the back of her hand. It was a white house, its paint faded and peeling, with a wrap-around porch, aging trees, and blue shutters. Her mother had insisted that they install new shutters a couple years before, so their blue paint was bright and cheerful against the aging background of the house. A waist-high picket fence wrapped around the large yard, providing unobstructed views to the river behind the house and the forest on both sides.

A warm feeling settled in the pit of Sarah's stomach. There was nothing better than the comfort of coming home.

"Glad one of us can get some sleep around here," Owen said with a wink. "Make sure you wipe that drool off my window before you get out."

Sarah gave him a baleful look. "I don't drool."

"No, but you do snore. Like a hibernating bear." He

dodged Sarah's fist when she tried to punch him in the arm. "Looks like the cleanup guys are back. Mom's been giving them hell since they started."

Sarah eyed the blue van in the driveway. "Yeah, I heard. Dad's office?"

Owen nodded. "I get it. He's only been gone for a few weeks. It's still an adjustment for all of us. I'm certainly not getting in her way."

"Because she'll direct her wrath at you?"

"Exactly." Owen parked the SUV and turned off the engine. "I was saving that lovely job for Mom's favorite child."

"Gee, thanks. I appreciate it." Sarah sighed. "I'll talk to her."

He grabbed her suitcase out of the back seat and hauled it inside while Sarah braved the basement to find their mother.

Mary stood inside her late husband's office, hands on hips. "Be careful with that bookshelf," she was saying when Sarah entered. "My husband built that himself twenty years ago. It's priceless."

Sarah wrapped her arms around her mother from behind and squeezed. Mary turned and hugged her back, smiling up at her. "There's my darling. How was your flight?"

"Great." Sarah cast a look at the two men holding a massive bookshelf between them. She knew them from high school, but she was too exhausted to remember their names. Everyone in La Conner knew each other; it was a typical small town. Her father's funeral a couple weeks before had literally been attended by every person in the city limits. Her parents were staples in the community; everyone knew their names. That was probably the only reason these guys were putting up with her mother's hassling.

"Mom, why don't we make some breakfast? I'm starving."

"Of course, sweetheart. Come on upstairs and we'll make some pancakes."

Sarah turned to follow her mother out of the room. As she turned the corner, she shot a thumbs-up at the two men in the office. They smiled and returned to their work, hassle-free.

* * * * *

After breakfast, Sarah found Owen in his study. She stood in the doorway and observed him at his computer, typing madly. His blond hair stuck up in all directions, the tips tinged blue with the light from his screen, and he had a look of intense concentration on his face.

"Owen."

Owen jumped and his hand jerked, nearly throwing his mouse off the end of the desk. He glared over his shoulder at her. "Don't scare me like that," he muttered, turning to look back at the screen. "Do you want me to die at the ripe age of 24?"

"Sorry." Sarah pulled up an extra chair and sat next to him. This brought back memories of high school. She'd spent hours sitting next to him in this same room, watching while he played video games. That was after he'd dropped out of school and spent all of his time online. He hadn't been speaking much at that point - which was strange, for Owen - and it was the only way she knew to support him.

Luckily, that phase hadn't lasted very long. Soon, Owen was back to his chatty self.

Sometimes her family joked that they wished Silent Owen would come back, especially when he was particularly mouthy toward anyone in particular, but Sarah didn't like to joke about that. She'd take Owen's jokes and sarcasm over his silence any day.

"What are you working on?" she asked, spinning her chair in a slow circle.

"New job for the guys. Just came in." Owen rubbed the back of his neck and rolled his shoulders. "As usual, I get all the hard work. I'm doing some preliminary research to see what we're up against."

"Research is the hard work? What about, I don't know, going out in the field and killing the bad guys?"

Owen snorted. "That's child's play. You try sitting at the computer for 27 hours straight and digging through miles of code to figure out someone's bank account number."

"Point taken. What's the job this time?" Sarah leaned forward, peering at the screen, but it was all mumbo jumbo to her.

"Sorry," Owen said, winking at her. "Classified."

"Seriously?" She scowled. "You know I'll be a part of ESI soon. I practically am after the last two weeks."

"Not if Emmett has anything to say about it."

"Emmett can shove it."

Owen laughed. "I'd like to see you tell him that to his face. What do you want? I know you didn't come to my lair because you missed me so much."

Sarah stopped spinning her chair, meeting her twin's eyes so he'd understand the seriousness of what she was about to say. "I did miss you, but that's not why I'm here. I need you to do me a favor, no questions asked."

"Oh no." Owen held up his hands. "Every time you ask me that, it usually ends in both of us getting into trouble. What is it this time? Do you need me to hack into NYU's system and change your grades? Because that's low, even for me."

Sarah ignored the jab about her grades and pulled the flip phone from her pocket, setting it on the desk in front of Owen's keyboard.

Owen picked it up and flipped it open. The screen blinked on and they both stared at the pin entry box. "What is this device? I haven't seen it since the stone age." His tone was joking, but his eyes were sharp when he glanced at her.

Sarah chewed her lip. How much should she say? She and Owen never kept secrets from each other, but she wasn't ready for the litany of questions she'd receive about Ryan.

She just wasn't ready for her family to know about it yet.

This was something she needed to handle on her own.

"It's a friend's. I don't know the pin, but I need access to the phone."

"Sounds like trouble. You know that's my middle name." Owen turned the phone over and opened the case, examining the battery. "Why do you need access to a sketchy old flip phone, though?"

"I just do. It's part of a favor for a friend."

"Right." Owen drew out the word, raising an eyebrow. "And I'm the Queen of England. Does this have something to do with why you left New York?"

Sarah folded her arms over her chest. "What part of no questions asked was hard for you to understand? Are you going to help me or not?"

Owen's green eyes narrowed on hers.

Sarah met his gaze with a glare. She really hoped she wouldn't regret asking for his help. Not that she had that much of a choice. There weren't very many computer geniuses in her circle.

"You're lucky I like you."

She released a breath and stood, pushing her chair back to the other side of the room. "Thank you. Let me know what you find. And Owen?"

"What?" He was already plugging the phone into a cord extending from his computer tower.

"Not a word to Emmett or Chance about this."

"That's not suspicious or anything." He smiled over his shoulder at her. "For the record, I don't like this. But I do like going behind Chance and Emmett's backs, so I won't say a word."

"Promise?"

He waved a hand, turning back to his screen. "I promise."

Sarah shot him a final warning look, even though he wasn't facing her to see it, and closed the door behind her as she left.

Relief made her knees weak. One less thing to worry about. If Owen made a promise to her, she could count on him to keep it.

Now all she had to do was wait.

CHAPTER 3

ROMAN STOMPED THROUGH THE DOORS of the ESI office. His expression probably looked as dark as his mood, but he didn't bother to hide it.

The rest of the team was sprawled in various chairs in the briefing room. The only sound in the room was the methodic "chink" of Cameron sharpening his hunting knife.

"Roman," Dominick said by way of greeting. He reclined in his chair, his booted feet resting on the coffee table next to his cowboy hat. "How was your personal time?"

Roman grunted and sat down in the chair between Dominick and Cameron.

"That good, huh?" Dominick grinned. "Where'd you go?"

"Had some personal things to take care of."

Cameron snorted, testing his blade with his thumb. His dark hair, a little long, fell forward, hiding his expression. He was the strong silent type, but he made up for his lack of words with a mind sharper than most gave him credit for.

There wasn't a situation he couldn't find a way into - or out of, depending on the circumstances. That's why Emmett had picked him as their tactical advisor.

Dominick rolled his eyes. "Yeah, I reckon that's the point of personal time."

The door swung open and Emmett entered the room. He was their boss - one of them - and built more like a tank than a man. His dark hair was cropped short in a military cut and he held himself stiff and upright, as if at any moment he'd be called to attention by a commanding officer. His gaze swept the room, coming to a rest on Roman.

Roman returned his steady look.

"Where's Owen?" Dominick asked. "Shouldn't his hiney be here for the briefing?"

"He's already been briefed, and he's working on preliminary research. We have a new assignment." Emmett picked up a remote off the coffee table and pointed it at the giant screen that dwarfed the wall. It blinked on, revealing a typed memo with the United States government seal at the top.

Dominick whistled, long and low. "Uncle Sam needs us on this one, huh?"

"Discretion is key here. Our reputation for taking care of things quietly has spread through the security community. That's why the government called us. This is going to be completely off-book; as far as anyone is concerned, we never received these orders."

"Must be big," Dominick said.

Cameron grunted in agreement. He set his knife on the table and folded his arms across his chest, his dark eyes narrowed on the screen.

"It is." Emmett hit a button and the TV flipped to a new image. A map of Mexico.

Roman's eyes skimmed over the Golden Triangle, the last place he'd visited in Mexico. A woman's scream echoed in the far reaches of his memory. He shivered and forced his eyes further south.

A red dot sat in the middle of the jungle. It was relatively near Acapulco, disputed territory for the Mexican cartels. They'd been fighting over that land for years.

Next to the map, a satellite image of the area revealed a cluster of buildings where the red dot was, surrounded by nothing but jungle for miles in every direction.

Roman leaned forward. If the government wanted covert, this was the place to do it. It was completely remote, isolated from reinforcements. The team could be in and out before anyone knew they were there.

"It's so big that they won't even tell us who we're after," Emmett said.

"How are we supposed to take someone down without knowing who they are?" Cameron asked.

"We're not taking them down. This is a reconnaissance mission." Emmett gestured to the screen. "All we know is the location. This compound is the target, deep in the Mexican jungle. Our job is to gather as much intel as we can. Uncle Sam picked us because of our reputation for discretion. We're small and they can claim no responsibility if something goes wrong. This is going to be in and out, no fooling around. Wheels up tomorrow at 0900."

Dominick looked at his watch. "Eighteen hours? Piece

of cake. I'll make sure the jet is packed, fueled, and ready to go."

Emmett nodded. "Owen sent a brief to all of you. Read up on the location and all the info Owen has been able to gather about the location. It's not much, but it's all we've got. Roman, my office. The rest of you are dismissed."

Cameron and Dominick cleared out while Roman followed Emmett down the hall. His office sat on the other end of the building.

Once the door was closed securely behind them, Emmett sat in the big leather chair behind his desk and leveled a look at Roman. "I don't like this assignment."

Roman took the seat across from him, nodding in agreement. "Not enough information."

"They're sending us in blind. I don't like facing an unknown enemy."

"Then why did you accept the job?"

Emmett ran a hand over his short hair, irritation coloring his features. "This company is still young. If we want to grow, we'll have to get our boots muddy. I don't like it, but I know the team is more than capable of handling it. If we weren't, I wouldn't accept the assignment. How was your trip?"

"Fine." The image of Ryan's bedroom, filled with boxes, flashed in Roman's mind. Fresh rage swept through him. He should've been the one to pack up Ryan's things.

He should've been the one to stop Ryan's death.

"Roman, you've been here for eighteen months. I know you're a man who likes his privacy and I respect that. I'm the same way, so I won't ask you any questions. But I hope you know that you can trust this team if you need anything."

Roman nodded his thanks. He didn't doubt Emmett's words, but he'd never ask for the team's help. Not with this.

There was only one man who hated Roman enough to target his brother, and that man was far more powerful than ESI.

Emmett rested his elbows on his desk and steepled his fingers, his gaze sharp on Roman's face. "I need you to know that you're a part of ESI now, which means you're part of a bigger unit. Anything personal for you is personal for us."

"I know." Roman swallowed.

Did Emmett know something? His expression seemed like he did, but how could he? Roman's past was long buried; he and Jeffries had made sure of that before he left special forces.

"Good." Emmett stood. The harsh lines of his face softened slightly, the closest he ever got to a smile. "As long as you know that. Get out of here. I've got a family dinner to get to."

* * * * *

Sarah sat on the floor in her father's office. It was empty now, aside from the industrial-sized fans blowing air to dry the carpet. It was still a little damp, and the moisture soaked through her jeans, but she didn't care.

In her mind's eye, she could see the office how it usually was, with floor-to-ceiling bookshelves spanning the length of one wall. Heavy textbooks filled the shelves, interspersed with military artifacts from her father's time in Vietnam. A display of patches from her father's uniform jacket, his dented canteen, and his service medal in a blue velvet display.

The heavy mahogany desk usually sat on the opposite wall, underneath the American flag in a glass frame.

How many times had Sarah sat on the floor in this exact spot, telling her father about the latest drama at school? She didn't even remember the things those girls did now, but she did remember her father's advice. No matter what the situation was, his advice was always the same.

There's no use worrying about the things you can't control, Sar-Bear. All you can control is your reaction to those things, so you focus on that.

His warm, deep voice echoed through her mind, so clear that she wondered if she had really imagined it.

She missed him so much that it hurt.

What would he say to her now? Would his advice still be the same?

She couldn't control the fact that Ryan was dead, but she could control how his death was remembered. It wasn't a simple mugging; her gut told her that. The authorities had already closed the case and judging by Roman's reaction when she'd asked about it, he wouldn't pursue it either.

If Sarah didn't do something, the person who killed Ryan would go free.

She couldn't let that happen.

The savory smell of pot roast wafted into the room, pulling her out of her thoughts. Mouth watering, she glanced at her phone; it was time for Sunday dinner.

Sarah got to her feet and left her father's office. Before she closed the door, she took one last look at the empty room. Her heart ached at the bare walls and wet carpet. No wonder her mother was having a hard time. The sight of it so empty just reminded her that her father would never be there again, muttering to himself as he read one of his textbooks.

Shaking herself, she closed the door and took the stairs two at a time to the upper floor.

The thing she'd missed most while living in New York was Sunday dinners with her family. It had been a tradition for as long as she could remember. Mary spent all day in the kitchen, preparing a meal that would feed the whole family. It didn't matter what everyone had going on that day; if they were in the same state, they were expected at the house by six o'clock.

"What's cooking?" Sarah asked as she entered the kitchen.

Mary smiled over her shoulder, stirring something in a pot on the stove. She was in her element. "Not until everyone gets here. Set the table, please."

Sarah grabbed some plates out of the cabinet and began setting the huge oak table in the dining room. It was older than she was, passed down from her great-grandmother. The scratched, faded surface showed its age, but Mary would never get rid of it. It was big enough to seat the whole family, including all the significant others Mary hoped they would someday have.

Only Chance had delivered on that so far.

The front door opened in the distance and her brothers' deep voices drifted into the house. Sarah listened to their footsteps heading in the direction of the living room. ESPN was also a Sunday tradition, but only for the males in the family.

A few moments later, Bellamy entered the dining room with glasses and silverware. "Hey," she said with a bright smile, setting her load down on the table. She shrugged out of her black leather jacket and set it on the back of her usual seat. "How was your flight?"

Sarah gawked at the white bandages covering both of Bellamy's arms. She'd only been released from the hospital a few days before. After the ordeal she'd been through, being kidnapped and almost killed, she looked surprisingly good. There was a light in her eyes that Sarah hadn't seen since they were children, before Bellamy disappeared at the age of fifteen. Chance and their rekindled romance definitely had something to do with that.

Sarah's chest constricted, and she bit her lip to stop her eyes from misting. She was so happy for her friend. "Uneventful," she said, clearing her throat. "I hate red-eyes. I can never sleep in those stupid seats."

Bellamy laughed. "Well, I'm glad you're back. Did you get everything packed at your apartment?"

"Not exactly."

"How come?"

Sarah sighed. It's not like she could tell Bellamy that some rude jerk — two of them, actually — showed up at her apartment and ruined her flow. Just the thought of Roman made her angry all over again. "It's a long story."

Bellamy gave her an inquisitive look, but she could take a hint. She and Sarah had been friends for a long time, and she knew Sarah well enough to see that she didn't want to talk.

Sarah grabbed the glasses and silverware Bellamy had brought and started distributing them around the table. "Are you sure you should be moving around? Maybe you should sit down."

Bellamy shook her head, her brows scrunching in disapproval. "Chance has been making me rest since I got home from the hospital. I'd rather help than sit around."

"Um, didn't they release you like three days ago?"

"Four." Bellamy winked. "I'm fine, really. A little sore, but nothing I can't handle. Besides, I really wanted to be here today. It's the first time we've all been together since... you know, everything. I have a feeling it will be a good night."

Sarah's eyebrows went up at the secret smile playing across Bellamy's lips. "What makes you say that?"

Bellamy's eyes twinkled. "Guess you'll have to wait and see."

Oh, she knew exactly what that meant. Her stomach did an excited little flip and she grinned in delight at Bellamy. She kept her silence, though, as they finished setting the table. She didn't want to ruin the surprise.

"Dinner's ready," Mary called a few minutes later. She, Sarah and Bellamy brought steaming dishes to the table.

Chance, Emmett, and Owen ambled into the room a few minutes later, sniffing the air and licking their lips. Chance plopped a kiss on top of Bellamy's head, ruffling her short hair, and helped her into a chair. Sarah felt a twinge of envy as she watched Bellamy beam up at him. Happiness like that seemed so out of reach for her right now, but she wanted it.

Once everyone was seated, they automatically joined hands and prayed over their meal, just like they did every Sunday. Everyone salivated over the pot roast, potatoes, and homemade rolls, and Mary preened as they sang her praises.

Sarah loaded up her plate. She'd learned young to be quick at mealtimes, or else her brothers would eat everything before she even took a serving.

"How does it feel to be home for good?" Chance asked Sarah as he spooned some mashed potatoes onto Bellamy's plate.

Sarah shrugged. "Like I'm back in high school." She smiled at her mother. "I'm happy to be here, though."

"What are your plans for school?" Emmett asked.

Here it was; the interrogation she'd been dreading.

Sarah shifted in her seat, keeping her eyes on her plate. "I'm taking a break."

Emmett frowned in disapproval. His expression reminded her so much of her father that Sarah's stomach dropped. "Why? You only have two years left and you'll have your doctorate. Why quit now?"

"Not that it's any of your business, but I want to be home right now. There's been a lot going on, and I feel like this is where I need to be."

His eyebrows lowered and he opened his mouth, no doubt to fire a high-and-mighty response.

"Chance," Bellamy interrupted. "Don't you have something you'd like to share with your family?"

Sarah shot her a grateful look, which she returned with a small smile.

Chance nodded, wiping his mouth with a napkin. "Actually, I do."

The table fell silent as everyone looked at him expectantly.

"This month has been tough," he said. "We lost Dad and then we had the storm that flooded the house." He paused, his expression darkening.

Was he thinking about their desperate search for Bellamy? She was kidnapped during the storm and thanks to the floodwaters, ESI had a hard time finding her - and an even harder time transporting her to a hospital. They'd almost lost her.

The thought still gave Sarah chills.

She'd never forget the way Bellamy looked when they found her. Judging by the way Chance's jaw clenched, he wouldn't either.

"But through all that, we also regained someone very important in our lives." Chance smiled at Bellamy. She beamed back.

Sarah glanced around the table at her family. Emmett was watching the couple with a small smile, his eyes warm. He'd already guessed where this was going.

Thank God that his feelings toward Bellamy had done a one-eighty. Things were rough when she first reappeared in their lives. Emmett hadn't trusted her, and it had caused a lot of unnecessary drama.

"Bella and I have been talking," Chance continued, using the nickname only he had for her. "It hasn't been that long since she's been back, but we both feel that it's the right time to do this."

"We all know what you're going to say," Owen interrupted. "Just say it already. You're adopting a puppy, right? We need a canine presence in this family."

Bellamy laughed and stood up. "No, we're getting married!"

The table erupted in a chorus of cheers and heartfelt congratulations. Bellamy held out her hand so everyone could admire the beautiful diamond ring on her finger.

"Man, I really wanted a puppy. But well done, bud." Owen clapped Chance on the back, then pointed at Emmett. "You owe me twenty bucks."

Emmett shrugged good-naturedly.

"Were you betting on whether we'd get married?" Bellamy asked. She looked like she was trying to decide whether she should be offended.

"No, we knew you would," Owen replied. "We were betting on when. Emmett thought it would be at least six months. I bet two."

Bellamy laughed. "I guess we beat both of you."

"Yeah, but I'm closest, so I win."

Sarah stood to hug Bellamy. If only her father were here to see this. He would be so thrilled to have Bellamy as part of the family. "I'm so happy for you," she murmured. "Nobody deserves this more."

Bellamy smiled as she pulled back, eyes bright. "This wouldn't have happened without you. I hope you know that."

Sarah shook her head. "You guys were meant to be together. I just helped things along."

Mary was crying as she interrupted them to give Bellamy a hug. "There's no one I would rather have as my daughter-in-law."

"Thanks, Mary." Bellamy sniffed. "I've always thought of you as my second mom."

"And you've always been my second daughter. Now it will be legal."

Bellamy wiped her eyes and grinned.

"When's the big day?" Owen asked Chance.

"We're not sure yet, but we want it to be soon."

"October tenth."

All eyes flew to Bellamy. Shocked silence descended over the group. Sarah almost laughed aloud at the stunned look on Chance's face.

"One month?" Owen asked. "As in, four weeks?"

"I don't even know if we can get a venue in that time frame –" Chance began.

"Then we'll go to the courthouse." Bellamy nodded firmly. "I've been waiting for ten years. I don't want to wait any longer."

A big grin split Chance's face. He grabbed Bellamy around the waist - mindful of her wounds, Sarah noticed - and lifted her into the air, spinning her around. "October tenth it is!" he shouted.

Everyone cheered their approval.

Once they all calmed down after the big news, the family returned to the table to finish dinner. Sarah thought her heart would burst from her chest in happiness as she watched Bellamy and Chance out of the corner of her eye.

She could only dream of having a relationship like theirs one day.

"You know," she said to Bellamy with a wink, "this means we need to go shopping for a certain white dress."

"Why yes, we do," Bellamy agreed. "I have no idea where to start though."

"I do. There's a cute little wedding boutique at the mall."

"Last time you went to the mall, it ended with Bellamy in the hospital," Owen said. "You sure you want to try that again?"

The color left Chance's face and his arm tightened reflexively around Bellamy's shoulders.

"I don't have any psychotic murderers after me at the moment, so I think we'll be okay," Bellamy said, patting Chance's hand.

On second thought, maybe the mall wasn't such a good idea. A pang of guilt made Sarah's palms sweaty. After all, it was her fault that Bellamy had gotten attacked last time.

She forced a confident grin, hoping no one saw her brief flash of guilt. "I won't let her out of my sight this time, I promise."

Owen shot her an apologetic glance. She should've known he would be able to read her. Before he could say anything, though, Bellamy interrupted. "Let's go tomorrow morning. Mary, do you want to come?"

"Sorry, my dear, I have some errands I need to run in the morning." Mary fiddled with her napkin, her smile not quite staying in place. "You'll have to send me pictures of the options."

"Done." Bellamy smiled at Sarah. "How's ten o'clock?"

"Perfect." Sarah glanced at her mother. Why didn't she want to go? This should be the highlight of her year. Chance was getting married!

"I heard you guys have a new assignment," Chance said, changing the subject. Obviously the men were sick of talking about wedding dresses.

Emmett nodded. "You were busy, so I didn't bother you with it. We leave tomorrow morning."

"Who are you taking?"

"Roman, Dominick, and Cameron."

Sarah's blood boiled all over again at the mention of Roman. So he'd returned from New York too. He must've caught a flight not long after hers. What had he been doing there? Obviously it wasn't to pack up Ryan's things, because Sarah took care of that already. Kind of.

Ryan.

What was she doing? She didn't have time to worry about Roman. She needed to stay focused on her reason for coming home - finding Ryan's killer.

"Where are you going?" she asked, shaking off her dark thoughts. "Can I help?"

Emmett looked at her like she was a paranoid schizophrenic who stopped taking her meds. "You're not a part of ESI."

"Oh come on, I'm practically part of the team after I helped with Bellamy's case. You can't deny that I was an asset."

Chance frowned. "That was a one-time thing, Sarah. There's a lot more that goes into fieldwork, and you're not properly trained for it."

"You belong in school," Emmett added firmly. "Not out risking your life."

"Why?" Her voice rose. "Because I'm a woman? Come on, Emmett, this isn't 1965. Feminism is alive and well, and women are just as capable as men."

"I don't care that you're a woman. You're my little sister, and you're not trained. You have no idea what type of people we deal with on a daily basis. Any one of them would do much worse than kill you if they ever got their hands on you."

Bellamy shifted closer to Chance, her expression troubled.

Sarah stood and placed her hands on the table. Fury made them shake. "I may not have military experience like you guys, but I'm more than capable of taking care of myself. I'm trained in mixed martial arts and I carry a gun with me at all times. I'm also a licensed EMT and I'm trained to handle medical emergencies in dangerous situations. Something that would be very helpful out in the field."

The room had gone silent. Everyone took turns staring at Sarah and awkwardly staring at their own plates.

Slowly, Emmett stood and leaned across the table until their faces were inches apart. His green eyes were rock hard. "This is not a debate," he said succinctly. "You are not joining ESI, and that's final."

Sarah gritted her teeth, fighting the urge to lunge across the table at her brother. She was dangerously close to losing control. This wasn't like her. Usually she was excellent at keeping her cool, especially where Emmett was concerned.

But not today.

Today, she was tired of feeling helpless.

Sarah straightened and glanced at Mary. "Sorry, Mom, but I think I've lost my appetite."

Without looking at anyone else, Sarah stalked from the dining room.

CHAPTER 4

SOMETHING ABOUT THE SOUND of wind whistling through the trees always calmed Sarah's nerves. She sat in a lounge chair on the back deck, a blanket wrapped around her to combat the early fall chill. Ryan's medical textbook rested open on her lap.

The sun had set about an hour ago and Emmett, Chance and Bellamy had left, but she couldn't bring herself to go back inside yet. Instead, she alternated between staring out at the darkness and paging through the textbook.

Ryan's familiar handwriting scrawled across the margins of most pages. He would've made a great doctor; his handwriting was already impossible to read. Sarah absently traced the lines with her finger, remembering the many hours they'd spent together in the library.

He would commandeer a whiteboard and drag it over to their table so he could draw complex anatomies and formulas. When Sarah gave up studying, opting to take a nap on her book instead, he would wake her up by throwing markers at her from across the table.

Without him, there's no way she would've made it through medical school.

She missed him.

The back door opened and Owen slipped outside. Sarah didn't look up, instead busying herself by reading a section about blood disorders.

Owen sat in the chair next to hers. He didn't say anything, seemingly content to sit there and look out into the darkness of the backyard.

Sarah let the silence stretch for a while, then sighed. "Did Mom send you out here?"

"No." A pause. "Yes. But I also wanted to check on you."

"Well, you can tell her I'm fine."

"Are you?"

Sarah snapped the textbook closed. He could see right through her; there was no point in lying. "Not really."

Owen scooted his chair so it was right next to hers. For once, his expression was serious. Sarah was the only person he ever showed this to. "What's going on with you? You've been acting weird since you came home. First you quit school-"

"I'm taking a break."

"Don't give me that crap. I know you. You have zero plans to go back. What's going on?"

Sarah stared out into the darkness. The moon reflected off the river in the distance, bathing the water in silver light. "I don't know," she said quietly. "Maybe I feel like being a doctor isn't the right path for me anymore."

"Why? You've wanted to be a doctor since we were little."

"No," she corrected him. "*Dad* wanted me to be a doctor since we were little. A stable, safe job where I could help people and make a decent living so I could take care of myself."

"You can't tell me you never wanted to."

She sighed. "Maybe I did. But lately, I feel like I won't be able to help people the way I want to."

"What makes you say that?"

Sarah looked up at him and held his gaze. She needed him to understand, needed *someone* to understand. "You guys treat me like I'm a spoiled princess, but I've been living on my own in New York for six years and I've been just fine. I've been an EMT for three of those years. We're called to the scene *after* the destruction. Our job is to clean up the mess left behind. Do you know how many people never actually make it to the hospital? A lot more than you'd think. I've watched them die in my arms and I couldn't save them."

Ryan's face, bloody and lifeless, flashed in her mind.

Sarah took a deep breath to steady her wobbly voice. "What you guys do with ESI… you get there before it happens. You save people before they need doctors."

"I get where you're coming from, Sar-Bear, I do. But even out in the field, that's not how it always works. Even though we try to save people, sometimes we're too late. It's just as difficult. You're going to see just as many people die in your arms."

"I know. Trust me, I understand that. But this is what I want. I'm not going to change my mind."

Owen put his arm around her and squeezed. "I'm sorry. I didn't realize you felt that strongly about it."

Sarah rested her head on his shoulder. Ryan's face flashed before her again, laying in the alley, bleeding from multiple stab wounds.

Sarah never wanted to feel helpless like that again.

"I know I don't have the same training that the rest of you do," she whispered. "I never joined the military, but I know I can help. My heart tells me this is where I need to be."

Owen gave her another squeeze. "I think you need to have this conversation with Emmett. He's just protective. We all are. You're our baby sister and none of us want to see you get hurt. And we all know Emmett can be an asshole when it comes to getting his way."

Sarah smiled a little. "Such an asshole."

Owen laughed. "Talk to him - without the yelling. Tell him what you just told me. He'll come around."

"Thanks."

"You're welcome, but I have a confession to make. I didn't come out here just to give you fantastic life advice." Owen straightened and reached into his pocket. "I've got something that might cheer you up."

"What?"

He pulled something out of his pocket and handed it to her. It was Ryan's secret phone. "It was a piece of cake to hack. Thank you, early 2000's."

Sarah took it from him, heart racing. This was it. Now she would finally have some answers. "What did you find out?"

"It's a burner phone, the early kind. These things barely have service anymore. I can't tell whose it was, but they were careful. All the call logs were deleted. It took me a while to recover them, but all the outgoing calls went to a single phone number."

"Really?" Sarah looked at the phone in her palm. Thank God Owen hadn't figured out who the phone belonged to. She'd mentioned Ryan to her family a few times over the years, mostly to argue with her father about her decision to move in with him, but he had never met her family. She and Ryan had never been more than friends, despite what her father had suspected, so she'd never seen the need to bring him home. That and the fact that he looked terrified the one time she'd asked.

"After some serious digging - and I mean *serious* digging - I was able to trace the phone number back to a name."

Sarah waited, letting him draw out the suspense.

"Altez." Owen dropped the name like it was a bomb. He stared at her, waiting for a reaction. "Does that mean anything to you?"

Sarah shook her head, staring at the phone like it would ring and give her the answers to a million questions running through her head. What did Ryan get himself into?

"I thought you might say that. I did some preliminary checking and the guy's like a ghost." Owen laced his fingers behind his head and leaned back in his chair, staring at the darkness beyond. "I couldn't find anything about him."

"That's okay," Sarah said quickly. "That's all I really needed."

Owen leveled a doubtful look at her. "I know you said no questions, but I really want to ask you all the questions."

"Good thing you promised not to. And that means no more digging beyond this." She didn't want him to find something that might lead him to alert Chance or, worse, Emmett. "It's kind of a dead-end anyway."

"Fine. Just because it's you, and you're my twin."

Sarah kissed him on the cheek. "Thank you. I really appreciate it."

"Uh-huh. Someday I'm going to call on you for a favor, and it's going to be a really nasty one. Like covering up a murder, or pantsing Emmett in front of everyone at the office. When that day comes, you'll remember this day. Because you owe me."

Sarah rolled her eyes. "Got it."

"Good. I've got a really nasty favor to think of, so I'm going to get to work." Owen winked at her and ambled back into the house.

Sarah watched him go, then let out the breath she hadn't realized she was holding. She hugged the phone to her chest.

Now it was time for the difficult part.

She needed to find out who Altez was and if he killed her best friend.

And she had to do it without ESI's help.

* * * * *

Owen returned to his man cave.

His twin sister was acting real shady lately.

First, Emmett recruited him to investigate Bellamy behind Chance's back. Now Sarah wanted him to research some random Altez guy behind Emmett's back.

Why was Owen always the one to get roped into these things? Here he was, minding his own business...

His gift for technology was turning out to be more of a curse.

Owen dropped into his computer chair and grabbed a deck of cards off his desk. He shuffled them back and forth in his hands, chewing on the inside of his cheek.

Sarah told him to stop digging, but that just wasn't his style.

Besides, if she was into something she shouldn't be, Owen would throw his loyalty out the window.

That... and his curiosity was too difficult to resist.

Owen wasn't kidding when he said this Altez guy was like a ghost. No social security number, bank account, mailing address, online presence, or phone number.

The only reason he'd found the name at all was because he listened to a series of recorded phone conversations, and one of the users mentioned Altez by name.

There weren't many people in the world who could avoid Owen's hacking skills. Even though Sarah had asked him to stop, it was a point of pride now.

He had to know who Altez was.

Looked like Owen was in for another sleepless night.

* * * * *

Sarah didn't sleep much that night. There was too much to think and obsess about.

How could she do more digging without Owen's computer expertise?

She couldn't. She didn't have the resources to pursue this on her own. That's why she'd decided to come home in the first place.

Maybe Owen was right; she could try talking to Emmett. There was a chance he'd understand if she just explained what was going on. Maybe he would help her.

By the time the sun rose and it was an acceptable hour to get up, Sarah got out of bed and threw on some new clothes. Yoga pants and a sweatshirt, same as yesterday, but these were a different color. Once her hair was pulled back into a ponytail and she'd laced her running shoes, she was ready to go.

Mary was standing at the stove when Sarah came downstairs. "Where are you off to so early?"

"I'm going to ESI," she said, grabbing a banana from the counter on her way across the kitchen. "I need to talk to Emmett before Bellamy and I go shopping."

"Oh, I almost forgot. Bellamy called this morning and said she'd like to go shopping tomorrow afternoon instead. Apparently something came up." Mary smiled. "I'm glad you're going to talk to Emmett. It's about time you two discussed what happened yesterday."

"Uh, yeah. That." Sarah cleared her throat. "Tomorrow's fine for shopping. Are you sure you don't want to come with us?"

"I'd love to, but I have some other things to do."

Mary's smile slipped. "I have to meet with the attorney over your father's will."

Sarah's stomach dropped. Mary's unwillingness to go shopping suddenly made sense. "Oh, I didn't realize. Do you want me to go with you? I'm sure Bellamy would understand."

Mary waved a hand, turning back to the stove. "No, honey, you go with Bellamy. I can handle it. Just take lots of pictures for me."

The tension in Mary's shoulders told Sarah she wouldn't be able to handle it as easily as she thought. Sarah made a mental note to let Owen know so he could go with her.

"Okay, if you're sure. Call me if you need anything. I love you." She kissed her mom on the cheek and left the house.

The ESI office was in downtown La Conner, about ten minutes from her house. It was a historic brick building on the outside, but the inside had been completely remodeled and updated. Chance designed it himself when he founded the company. He talked about it to anybody who would listen.

Sarah breezed through the front door as if she owned the place. By extension, she kind of did.

Chance would probably get a kick out of that. She'd have to tell him later.

There wasn't a formal reception area. Instead, the doors opened into a lounge with comfy-looking leather chairs and a television on the wall. It was all very masculine. No wonder they didn't have any female members. She could choke on all the testosterone in the building.

The team sprawled in the lounge chairs, dressed in full tactical gear. Sarah's eyes skimmed over Cameron and Dominick, landing squarely on Roman. He sat in the chair closest to the door, examining an assault rifle in his lap. Awareness prickled at the back of her neck when his head lifted and his eyes met hers.

If he was surprised to see her, he didn't show it. His eyebrows lowered and he pinned her with an intense gaze.

Sarah's stomach did a little flip.

Why did he affect her so much?

"Hey there," Dominick drawled. He sat in the chair across from Roman, arms spread over the back of the chair. A cowboy hat rested on his lap.

Sarah yanked her gaze from Roman's and smiled at Dominick and Cameron, who was sitting next to him. "Hi," she said brightly. "What are you guys up to?"

"Just getting ready to head out." Dominick placed the hat on his head. "Very important mission today, you know."

"Oh?" Sarah tried her best to look uninterested. "What is it?"

"Reconnaissance." He winked. "Requested by Uncle Sam himself."

"What for?"

"A secret base of some secret cartel in Mexico." Dominick grinned. "Spy stuff."

"Top secret stuff," Cameron murmured, shooting Dominick a quelling look.

Sarah shifted her stance and glanced around the room again. She could feel the weight of Roman's gaze. "Got it.

Where's Emmett?"

"In his office."

"Thanks." She smiled. "Good luck with your top-secret mission."

Sarah headed down the hall, studiously avoiding Roman's eyes. She passed a conference room and two more offices, one of which was full of wall-to-wall computer screens. That was Owen's space, not that he spent much time there. He preferred to work in his man cave at the house; he said his hacking muse never left there.

When she finally reached Emmett's door, she knocked and waited for him to call out before she entered.

Emmett sat at a huge mahogany desk. His office was decorated minimally, with a single bookcase and two chairs facing his desk. The walls were bare except for a Purple Heart medal and certificate he'd received during his time in the military. He'd never told anyone what happened on his last mission, but he was hospitalized for two months afterward.

Emmett looked up as she entered. His eyebrows rose, but otherwise he didn't move. "What are you doing here?"

Sarah wiped her sweaty palms on her pants. She shouldn't be scared to talk to her own brother. Ryan's voice echoed in her head, telling her to "woman up" and get it done.

She sat in one of the chairs facing him. "The guys said you're leaving on a mission today," she said instead of answering his question. She needed a second to compose herself.

Emmett nodded, straightening a stack of papers in

front of him. "We leave in ten minutes."

"Where to?"

"Mexico. We've been contracted by the U.S. government for a fact-finding assignment."

Wow, he was actually talking to her. She could do this. "Will it be dangerous?"

Emmett raised an eyebrow. "It's an unsanctioned operation by the government. If we're caught or imprisoned for any reason, they will deny knowledge of us or our objective. But in terms of the likelihood that we'll see combat this time? Not likely."

"Oh." Sarah shifted in her seat.

"Sarah. Why are you here?" His voice turned flat, his patience wearing thin.

"I wanted to apologize."

"Apology accepted. Is that all?"

"No." Sarah struggled to keep her voice even. She was doing her part; why wasn't he apologizing for being a complete jerk last night? "I came because I wanted to tell you that I really am serious about joining ESI."

"I already told you it's not happening. End of discussion." Emmett stood and grabbed his jacket off the back of his chair.

Sarah stood too and moved in front of him, blocking his path to the door. "Listen to me. If I could just explain-"

"I thought I made myself clear. You don't have what it takes to join this unit. I won't put my team's lives in danger because you want to run around playing hero."

"That's not what I-"

"Sarah, I won't tell you again."

"Will you just listen to me for one second?" Sarah snapped. "How about you let me explain before you tell me no?"

Emmett grunted in exasperation and folded his arms across his chest. "I'm listening."

The expression on his face told her that he wasn't interested in hearing what she had to say.

Sarah took a step back, humiliated that she felt the sting of tears. She bit her lip. They were tears of anger. Right?

"You know what? Never mind."

If he didn't want to help her, she'd do it by herself. She didn't need him.

Sarah spun on her heel and stomped out of his office. "Good luck on your assignment," she threw over her shoulder as she exited.

Emmett didn't follow her.

The last thing she wanted to do was face the team, so she took a detour into the bathroom and locked the door behind her. Standing in front of the mirror, she scrunched her face into weird expressions, trying to tamp down her rising emotions. Her breathing hitched and she slapped a hand over her mouth to muffle the sound.

She was never going to find Ryan's killer this way.

Sarah leaned her forehead against the mirror, grateful for the coolness against her flushed skin. Somewhere deep down, she knew that Emmett was just doing what he thought was best. He was worried about her intentions, that she would jeopardize the team he'd spent a long time building.

If only he would *look* at her, not as a team leader, but as a brother. Just for one second. Then maybe he would understand.

But that would never happen. Emmett didn't work that way.

Sarah sighed. She could go to Chance for help, but he had a bride-to-be to spend time with. And a wedding to plan. Besides, he'd been through enough. She couldn't drag him into another potentially dangerous situation.

Owen was also out of the question. He may have the resources she needed, but ultimately he worked for Emmett. If there was even a hint that this might be dangerous - which she suspected it was - then he would run straight to Emmett.

There was only one other person who could help.

Sarah pulled her phone out of her pocket and scrolled through her contacts. There it was. Tom Hansen. She hadn't spoken to him in years, but he had connections. And he owed her a favor.

She had to try. For Ryan.

Decision made, she felt a little better, but she still had no intention to face Emmett or the team again. She waited ten more minutes to make sure they were gone before she unlocked the bathroom door.

When she opened it, however, she found Roman leaning against the wall on the opposite side of the hallway. His arms were folded across his chest, his booted feet crossed at the ankles.

Sarah's heart skittered in her chest. She surreptitiously swiped at her eyes, hoping he wouldn't guess what she'd been doing in there for so long.

Roman's eyes didn't miss a thing. He pushed away from the wall and towered over her, taking in her expression with his shrewd gaze.

Sarah felt her cheeks flush and cursed her light complexion. "What are you doing?" she demanded. "Aren't you supposed to be on a plane by now?"

Roman didn't answer at first. Instead, his eyes narrowed and he continued to look at her as if she was some science experiment he was trying to figure out.

Sarah swallowed hard. Her eyes went to his scar and she wondered how he got it. It slashed through his eye and down his cheek. For some reason, it made him look like a pirate.

If she'd been in a better mood, she would've laughed at the mental image of him with a parrot on his shoulder.

"Why did you come here?" he asked.

"Not that it's any of your business, but I needed to talk to Emmett about some things."

"Were you trying to convince him to let you join ESI?"

Sarah's eyebrows shot up.

"He didn't agree with it when we were trying to find Bellamy, and I bet he doesn't agree with it now."

Sarah gritted her teeth. The only reason Emmett had let her ride along to find Bellamy was because Roman had recommended it. That was after he kissed her in this very hallway. "What do you care?"

"Why do you want to join?"

The question took her aback, and she could only stare at him. One minute he was a condescending jerk, and the next he acted like he actually cared.

If he did care, he'd be out there looking for Ryan's killer.

If it was Owen, Chance, or even Emmett, as much as he annoyed her, Sarah would be doing everything in her power to find the one who did it. That's what family did.

"Why are you going on this assignment?" she asked. "Why aren't you out there looking for Ryan's killer?"

His lips thinned. "I'm doing all I can."

"Really? Because it looks like you're not doing anything at all." Sarah paused, eyes narrowing. "I've already got a lead. Does the name Altez mean anything to you?"

Roman's expression flashed with something other than his usual stoic-ness. "No."

He was lying. He knew something, and he still wasn't doing anything about it.

Fine. She didn't need Emmett's help, and she certainly didn't need Roman's help.

Sarah started to storm past him, but his hand touched her shoulder. His fingers were warm through the material of her sweatshirt, and she felt goosebumps rise on her flesh. She looked down at his hand and then back up to meet his eyes.

"Is that why you're doing this? Because of Ryan?" His gaze examined every inch of her face. "You're putting yourself in danger for nothing. Ryan's dead. You can't help him now."

Sarah shook off his hand and shoved him hard in the chest. Roman stumbled back a few steps, looking surprised. "Don't act like you know me. I don't answer to you or to anyone else. If I don't do something about Ryan's death, it's obvious nobody will." She gave him a disdainful look and turned away, walking fast toward the exit.

She half expected him to follow her, but he didn't.

* * * * *

Roman watched Sarah's retreating form. He still felt her hands on his chest like he'd been permanently branded. Her words echoed in his head.

If I don't do something, nobody will.

Roman looked down at his hand. It was outstretched like he wanted to call her back. He curled his fingers into a fist and forced it down to his side. What could he even say?

To her, he looked like a heartless prick.

Roman gritted his teeth and stalked off toward the supply room to grab the walkies that Dominick had forgotten.

Sarah didn't know what she was getting herself into. She was so far over her head that she was going to drown before she even realized she was supposed to be swimming.

How had she found Altez's name so quickly?

After Bellamy's rescue, he shouldn't underestimate Sarah's abilities. Clearly she was more than capable of getting herself into trouble.

Altez was not a man to trifle with. If he found out about Sarah's little investigation, he would kill her.

She was throwing a serious wrench in Roman's plans. He needed to do something about it, before she did something stupid and got them both killed.

Roman grabbed the set of walkies and hurried out to

where the rest of the team was waiting in the SUV.

CHAPTER 5

SARAH DIDN'T GO STRAIGHT HOME. Instead, she continued into the heart of downtown and pulled into a parking spot in front of the police station. She was still rattled from her encounter with Roman.

What was he thinking when he looked down at her like that? If Ryan were here, he could explain it to her. He always had a sense of what other people's motivations were.

Sarah got out of her Jeep and looked up at the police station, urging her feet to go inside before she could change her mind.

She approached the woman at the front desk and smiled politely. She didn't recognize her; she must be new to town. "Is Tom Hansen in?"

"Can I tell him who's asking?"

"Sarah Erickson. I'm an old friend."

"Just a minute." The woman looked bored. She got up and disappeared into the back of the office. Sarah waited impatiently, rocking back and forth on her heels as she watched people passing by on the street outside.

"Sarah 'Smarty-Pants' Erickson."

Sarah looked up. Tom stood in the doorway, grinning. He was a few years older than her, closer to Emmett's age, but they'd dated briefly in high school while she was a freshman. The department had been good for him. He'd always been a little on the husky side when they were in school, but he'd leaned out. His sandy blond hair was short and he had a bit of a receding hairline already, but he was still handsome.

"Tom," Sarah said, smiling, and gave him a hug.

He dropped a kiss on the top of her head, just like he always used to do when they were in high school. "I haven't seen you in years. What are you doing back in town? Are you a fancy doctor yet?"

Sarah's smile slipped. She ducked her head under his shoulder and wrapped her arm around his waist. "Can we talk in your office?"

Tom's grin didn't waver. "Of course. Come on in."

The receptionist glowered at Sarah as she passed by the front desk. Sarah resisted the urge to stick her tongue out at the lady. She followed Tom through the maze of cubicles and into the back of the building. His office was only half the size of Emmett's, but it was comfortable and tidy, with a few knick-knacks on the desk.

"How have you been?" Sarah asked, perching on the end of the hard chair facing Tom's desk. "How's Jennifer?"

Tom smiled blissfully at the mention of his wife. "Jen's great. We just bought a house last year. Thinking we'll start a family soon."

"Wow, you haven't done that yet? I thought you'd

have like eight kids by now."

Tom laughed. "Jen would love that. No, we were waiting until I was more settled here at the station. Now I'm feeling like we're finally ready."

"Congratulations." Sarah couldn't help but smile at the happiness in Tom's eyes. Once upon a time, she'd wanted to marry him, but they'd gone their separate ways after graduation. It never would have worked. Besides, judging by the goofy grin he wore at the mere mention of his wife, she was obviously his perfect match. How could Sarah not be happy for him?

Tom leaned back in his chair. "Not that it's not great to see you, but what do you want?"

Sarah laughed. "What makes you think I want something? Maybe I just missed you and wanted to say hi."

"That's a nice gesture, even though it's a lie." He winked. "I know that look in your eye. It's the one that always got us into trouble. Want to tell me why you're really here?"

Sarah crossed her legs, doing her best to look innocent. "Remember that time when you let a pig loose in the high school gym for your senior prank? And they almost didn't let you graduate?"

"Yeah, you took the blame. You said you still had three years ahead of you and they couldn't stay mad forever."

"Right. And you said you owed me one."

"Okay...?"

"I've come to collect."

Tom chuckled. "All right, but you know I'd help you even if I didn't owe you a favor. All you have to do is ask."

"Thanks. But this is kind of a big deal." Sarah pulled a piece of paper out of her pocket and unfolded it. She slid it across the table to Tom.

He picked it up, examining the name she'd scrawled inside. "Altez." He looked up at her. "Okay. Who is he?"

"That's what I need to find out."

He raised an eyebrow. "I'm happy to help, but why aren't you asking Owen or one of the others to look into this? They probably have more resources than I do."

"Let's just say, they wouldn't be willing to help. Besides, this is kind of personal." Sarah looked away. "I need to handle it myself."

"Are you in some kind of trouble?" Tom's brown eyes pierced hers.

"No, of course not," Sarah said quickly. "Nothing like that. I just want to know what you can find out about this guy. Can you look into it for me?"

Tom frowned down at the name. "All right. Give me a couple of days. There are a couple databases I can check."

"Thank you."

"Sarah," he said, his expression turning serious. "You promise me that you're not getting into trouble. Your brothers will kick my ass if you get hurt and I let it happen."

"Cross my heart. Will you call me when you find something?"

"Sure."

Sarah hugged him goodbye and left the station. Hopefully giving Tom that name wouldn't come back to bite her. The more people who knew, the more likely it would get back to Emmett or Chance. Then she'd have a CIA-level interrogation on her hands, complete with waterboarding.

She had to trust that Tom would respect their friendship and do as she asked.

* * * * *

Roman stood in the ESI parking lot, watching as the SUV with his team drove away.

Emmett wasn't thrilled with his decision to pass on this assignment. Actually, that was an understatement. His exact words were, "You and I are going to have a long, painful conversation about this when I get back."

Roman had 24 hours to find some answers and put a stop to Sarah's digging before shit hit the fan.

Emmett was done with vague responses to his questions. He would expect a full explanation, and Roman would have no choice but to give it to him.

Roman pulled out his cell phone on his way back into the office.

Jeffries answered on the first ring. "Hello?"

"Jeffries, it's Roman."

"Holt, how are you? Any news?"

Roman set his go-bag in the supply room and returned to the lounge to pace in front of the screen. "I've got a problem. Is your team still looking for our mutual friend?"

Jeffries wasn't dull. He caught on to Roman's meaning immediately. "No, but I've been keeping tabs. Why?"

"Emmett's little sister was Ryan's roommate. She's looking into his death and digging where she shouldn't be."

"Shit," Jeffries said. "What do you need from me?"

"I need everything you have on our mutual friend. I'm going to do some digging of my own and see if I can get to the bottom of this."

"Sure. I'll send it over as soon as I get home. Roman... be careful. Keep an eye on the girl. If she's digging, you can be sure he knows about it. She could be in danger."

"Roger. Thanks, Jeffries."

"Keep me in the loop."

"Will do." Roman hung up and dropped his cell phone on the coffee table. With a big sigh, he rolled his shoulders to relieve some of the tension building up there.

If anyone could help him track down Altez, it was Jeffries.

Their team was disbanded after their failed attempt to capture Altez five years ago, but Jeffries wasn't the type to give up so easily. He'd been in special forces long enough that he had a lot of contacts who owed him a favor. Just as Roman had suspected, he still kept up on the latest intel about Altez's activities.

Hopefully it would help Roman determine if Altez had anything to do with Ryan's death. His gut told him that Ryan's death wasn't an accident, but Altez was more powerful – and smarter – than even the U.S. government. They'd been trying to capture or kill him for years with no success.

Roman grabbed his keys and headed for the parking lot. While he waited for Jeffries to send him the intel he needed, he might as well make himself useful.

There was a certain woman who was determined to get herself into trouble, and Roman was the only one who could stop her.

* * * * *

Pioneer Market hadn't changed since Sarah shopped there with her mother when she was young. The faded red and green sign still boasted "Fresh Produce & Meats," and the same family still owned it and worked as cashiers.

Sarah glanced at her phone as she entered the store. Mary had sent her a list of groceries to get for dinner.

She couldn't even remember the last time she set foot in a grocery store.

In New York, she either ate out or had groceries delivered. Grocery stores were few and far between, and way too crowded for her liking.

Sarah walked down the baking aisle. "Ghee, ghee..." She scanned the shelves. "What *is* ghee, anyway?"

"It's clarified butter," a deep voice said from behind her.

Sarah whirled around.

Roman stood a few feet away.

"What the..." She blinked at him. "What are you doing here?"

Roman held up a gallon of milk, as if that answered her question.

"No, I mean... Aren't you supposed to be on assignment with the rest of the team?"

"I had some things to take care of." His intense gaze met hers.

Her stomach did a little flip. "Uh, what things?"

He shrugged. "Just things."

"Right. That really clears things up. If you'll excuse me…"

"The ghee is in the next aisle over," Roman said as she walked away. "Want me to show you?"

"I'm perfectly capable of finding it myself," she called back.

His long legs caught up to her easily. "Sure, but it doesn't hurt to ask for help."

"I don't need your help."

"Are you sure?"

Sarah stopped walking and glared up at him. "Why do you keep popping up everywhere? Are you stalking me or something?"

Roman raised an eyebrow. "Purely coincidence. Actually, I was here first. I'd say *you're* the one following *me*."

Sarah opened her mouth to reply, but she couldn't come up with something witty to say. So she closed it and kept walking.

"Aren't you going to get your ghee?"

"Forget the ghee," she snapped, and walked right out the front door.

Screw groceries. Her mom could come get them later, or Sarah would order them on Amazon.

Roman's laughter followed her out the door.

* * * * *

Sarah stewed the whole way back to the house.

Who did Roman think he was?

She couldn't figure him out. One moment he was mysterious and brooding, and the next he was teasing her. First he was kissing her, then he completely ignored her.

Why didn't he go on assignment with the team?

Just thinking about him gave her a headache.

When Sarah pulled up to the house, the cleanup crew was just leaving. "How'd it go?" she called as she hopped down from her Jeep. She recognized a few of the men from high school.

A lot of people who grew up in La Conner never left. It was that kind of town.

"Good," one man called back. She couldn't remember his name, but they'd taken a math class together once. "The basement is all cleaned. You're good to start putting your stuff back to the way it was."

If only everything could go back to the way it was. Her father and Ryan would still be alive and Sarah would be in the middle of the fall semester at NYU, instead of sneaking around behind her brothers' backs trying to solve a murder.

Sarah forced the thought away and waved as the van pulled out of the driveway.

She found her mother right where she expected to, in her father's office. Stacks of unopened boxes teetered around the room. It was eerily similar to the way Sarah's apartment had looked when she was packing up Ryan's stuff.

Mary stood next to the bookshelves, an open box at her feet. She was busy returning heavy books to their places.

"Hey, honey," she said, catching sight of Sarah. "Did you get the groceries I asked for?"

"Uh, no. Sorry. I ran into someone really annoying at the store and didn't end up grabbing anything."

Mary raised her eyebrows. "Someone annoying?"

"Never mind. Need some help?"

"Sure. You know where everything goes."

Sarah opened another box and lifted out a set of bookends. They were heavy brass, carved into the head of an eagle. She bit her lip at the pang of homesickness. Not for the house, but for the home she remembered. Hours sitting in this study with her father, listening as he told her stories from his days in the military. Asking him for advice about the dumbest teenage things. Laughing at his dad jokes for the millionth time.

That was a version of home that she'd never get back.

"He loved those." Mary gently took the bookends from Sarah's hands, examining them.

"Yeah." Sarah's throat was tight.

"You know, he'd probably want you to have them. Maybe you can put them in your own office someday."

Sarah took them back, swallowing hard, and placed them on the shelf where her father had always kept them. "I don't think so."

Mary let the silence linger for a moment. "I know you don't want to talk about New York, but it would be nice if you told me why you don't want to go back to school."

Sarah didn't even bother telling her that she was just taking a break. Everyone knew she was lying. "Something bad happened, Mom," she said quietly. "It made me realize that maybe I don't want to be a doctor anymore."

Mary looked at her for a long time. She could have

asked for details, but she didn't. Sarah loved her for that. "Whatever happened, is it enough to make you give up on your dream?"

Sarah eased herself into her father's desk chair and slowly spun in a circle. "I don't think it was ever really my dream," she admitted. "Dad has been telling me since I was little that I would make a great doctor. It was always our thing. I heard it for so long that I started to believe it was my dream. I wanted to do as he suggested and make him proud." She paused and bit her lip. "Now he's not even here to see it, you know?"

Mary sighed and leaned against the edge of the desk. Her eyes were wet. "Your dad always wanted you kids to follow his example, that's true. But whether you become a doctor or not, you've already done that. All four of you have followed in his footsteps. He always believed in helping people, and you do that every day. As an EMT, or as a part of ESI. It's the same thing." She placed a hand over Sarah's and squeezed. "Ultimately your dad wanted you to be happy. If pursuing something other than medicine will make you happy, then that's what you need to do."

"Thanks, Mom." Sarah smiled shakily and wiped a tear that had escaped down her cheek. "You always know what to say."

"That's a mother's job." Mary touched Sarah's cheek, her expression turning serious. "Here's another piece of motherly advice. Our family is strongest when we rely on each other. I relied on you kids when your dad got sick. Chance relied on you when Bellamy went missing. And whatever bad thing happened in New York, you can overcome it if you rely on us. You've always been very independent, but you can't take on everything by yourself. Remember that, okay?"

Sarah's stomach twisted into a knot. Her mother saw right through her, just as she always did. "Okay. I'll remember."

CHAPTER 6

EMMETT CROUCHED with his gun at the ready. His camouflage gear blended easily into the jungle.

Cameron and Dominick fanned out, skirting the perimeter of the compound.

It would be radio silence until they reached their assigned observation points.

Emmett was alone with the jungle and his thoughts.

Sweat dripped down his neck, soaking his shirt.

Damn humidity.

When ESI grew, Emmett would choose missions *away* from Mexico. Away from jungles in general, actually.

He hated the jungle with every fiber of his being.

Too many memories.

The humidity was thick, threatening to choke him.

"I've reached my zone," Cameron's quiet voice said into the radio. "All quiet."

"Same here," Dominick reported. "Wall's about

thirteen feet high if I had to guess. Three guards in each tower."

"Automatic weapons mounted in each direction," Cameron added. "It won't be an easy entry."

"Good thing that's not our assignment," Emmett said. "Can either of you see inside?"

"I got a glimpse when the gate opened," Dominick said. "There's a whole lotta people in there, but most of them look half-starved. Every one of them is carrying a weapon though."

Emmett wiped the sweat from his brow. "Good report. Continue to observe. Radio silence until I give the word."

"Roger."

"Yes sir."

Emmett shifted, eyeing his area of the wall. The concrete looked thick and solid. It would take a good amount of C4 to blow a hole in it.

The best entry would be from the sky, but without getting into the compound, Emmett couldn't begin to guess what kind of air defenses they might have.

Not to mention the four guard towers. If they were vigilant enough to watch the inside of the compound as well as the outside, an air entry would be suicide. The team would be riddled with bullet holes before they reached the ground.

There was only one gate into the compound, and it was manned by six armed guards at all times.

A blast entry was the only option.

"How's it going down there?" Owen said in Emmett's ear.

"Nothing to report yet. How are things there?"

Owen snorted. "Oh, you know. Sarah's hulking out about you not letting her join the team. She's off somewhere doing God-knows-what. I haven't seen her all day."

"Mm."

Emmett's stomach lurched when he thought of their argument in his office.

He'd been callous.

She hated him now, but someday she would thank him. The things Emmett and the rest of the team had seen... Sarah didn't need experiences like that on her conscience.

Having her in the field would be a colossal mistake.

Mental strain aside, Emmett knew his team. Any one of them would risk his life to save Sarah's. They would do the same for anyone on the team, but they all had a soft spot for women. It could be detrimental on an assignment if that clouded their better judgment.

Emmett wouldn't be able to live with himself if something happened to Sarah or one of his teammates because Emmett let her join.

They worked better as an all-male unit.

Some might call it sexist. Emmett didn't care.

Sarah was his little sister, and he didn't want her to get hurt.

"You're awfully quiet," Owen said. "Are you re-thinking your life choices?"

"No."

"Did Sarah tell you *why* she wants to join the team?"

She'd tried. Emmett had shut her down before she

could.

"It doesn't matter why. She would be a liability in the field."

A loud sigh, like a big whoosh of static, sounded in Emmett's ear. "Bro, sometimes you're so dense it physically hurts me."

Emmett grunted.

"No, seriously, I think I have a bruise from your stupidity. Want me to send you a picture of it? It's right next to my—"

"Enough, Owen," Emmett snapped. "I'm in the middle of an operation. Radio silence."

Owen snorted. "Yes, sir."

Emmett gritted his teeth, tamping down the urge to rip the earpiece out.

He didn't have time to worry about Sarah right now.

"One more pass," he said to Cameron and Dominick. "Look for any weak points we can report to Uncle Sam. Once that's done, let's get the hell home."

* * * * *

The next afternoon, Bellamy was out the door and bouncing down the steps before Sarah even put the Jeep in park. Chance poked his head out the front door and yelled something, grinning. Bellamy ran back up the steps to give him a kiss and he waved as she finally hopped into the passenger seat.

"Sorry," Bellamy said, breathless. "I was so excited that I forgot my wallet."

Sarah hid a smile. She'd grown used to the edgy, moody woman Bellamy had become, but lately she'd begun showing glimpses of the girl she used to be. It was like just admitting her feelings for Chance had lifted the world off her shoulders.

Bellamy caught Sarah staring and raised an eyebrow. "What? Do I have egg on my face or something?"

"No, sorry. I was zoning out. Where to?"

Bellamy pulled a piece of pink paper out of her purse and unfolded it. A beautiful woman in a flowing silk gown smiled from the page, almost dwarfed by the gaudy lettering declaring some type of sale. "It's this boutique called Bradley's," Bellamy said. "Your mom said they're really good, and I guess Chance heard it from some ladies in town too."

"Chance talked to the ladies in town about wedding dresses?" The mental image of her big, muscular brother asking for wedding dress advice was too much. Sarah snorted.

Bellamy's eyes twinkled. "Apparently he's quite the Chatty Kathy when he goes grocery shopping."

Sarah laughed. "All right, the mall it is. Let's do this."

La Conner wasn't a big city. By "mall," Sarah really meant the small strip mall in the center of town. Unlike the mall where Bellamy had been kidnapped, this was in La Conner's city limits. It was in the touristy section, if there was such a thing, one in a number of quaint shops that bordered the river. Sarah found a parking spot just down the street, only a block away from the ESI headquarters.

Bradley's was a lot bigger on the inside than it looked.

Wedding dresses in plastic bags lined the walls in organized rows. Toward the back of the shop was a dressing room with a small circular platform and mirrors on three sides.

Lucky for them, the shop was pretty much deserted. There were only so many brides in La Conner, and none of them shopped for wedding dresses on a Tuesday morning.

Bellamy bounced with excitement. Sarah couldn't help but laugh as they wandered up and down the rows, picking out dresses that Bellamy liked. She was like a kid in a candy store.

"So how has everything been?" Sarah asked her. "Since your uncle and everything."

"Good, actually." Bellamy picked up another dress and handed it to Sarah, who obediently slung it over her arm. If they picked out any more, Sarah might collapse under the weight. "Can I tell you a secret?"

"Oh, you know I love a good secret. Spill it."

"Since Governor Powell's illegal dealings became public knowledge, the criminal sector of Portland is in upheaval. Chance says I'll be able to use my contacts to help ESI. I still know a lot of people who would be willing to trade information, which will come in handy with some of ESI's assignments."

"Chance is letting you help ESI?" Sarah scowled. "What am I, chopped liver? I can bring valuable skills to the table."

Bellamy looked taken aback. "I'm sorry, I didn't mean to hurt your feelings."

"My feelings aren't hurt. I'm pissed, but not at you." Sarah huffed. "I have a bone to pick with my protective older brothers."

"If it makes you feel any better, there's no way Chance will let me anywhere near anything dangerous." Bellamy sighed. "I've lived my whole life with danger on my doorstep, and I learned how to take care of myself a long time ago. It's a little difficult to handle all the coddling."

"I know the feeling." Sarah rolled her eyes.

Wait a second...

"You said you're still in contact with your criminal friends in Seattle?"

Bellamy's brow wrinkled. "Yes. Why?"

Sarah bit her lip. "Do you think I could ask you for a favor?"

"Anything. What's up?"

"I'm looking for some information on someone. A friend of mine back in New York... I think he got involved in something he shouldn't have. But I only have a name to go on."

"... And you want me to check with my contacts to see if anyone knows it."

"Without a word to Chance."

Bellamy grinned. "I'm always up for a good undercover operation. I'll reach out and see what I can find."

A huge weight lifted off of Sarah's shoulders.

She may not be able to ask Owen or Emmett for help, but it was nice to know she still had people in her corner.

"You're the best. Speaking of you... How are you doing? Like you, personally?"

Bellamy paused, as if debating what she would say next. "Honestly, I've been having nightmares about what happened. Chance wants to get me in to see a therapist to make sure I can talk through everything."

Sarah kept her expression bland. Of course Bellamy was having nightmares. Any normal person would. She'd gotten so used to seeing Bellamy's happiness lately that she hadn't considered what was going on behind the scenes.

"But really, I feel better than I have in a long time," Bellamy said. "Chance makes me feel safe, and I love being a part of your family."

"You are. Even without Chance, you're still an Erickson." Sarah shifted the massive pile of dresses to her other arm and shook the offended body part to get her blood flowing again. "Okay, no more heavy talk. We need to try these on before my arms fall off."

Bellamy laughed, and Sarah followed her toward the dressing room.

"You're amazing, you know," she blurted.

"How come?" Bellamy glanced over her shoulder, clearly puzzled by the outburst.

"You've faced so many trials in your life, and you've overcome every single one. I don't know how you do it."

Bellamy smiled. "Not without a lot of help. I wouldn't be here today if it wasn't for Sam and Chance. And you and your family."

"Do you miss Sam?" With the whirlwind of events since Bellamy entered their lives, Sarah had almost forgotten that she had lost her best friend recently too. Sam was murdered by Bellamy's uncle.

Did Bellamy feel the same pain that Sarah had been struggling with since Ryan's death?

"All the time." Bellamy sighed. "I wish she was here to

see this. She'd never believe that I'm getting married."

"I'm sure she'd be so happy for you."

"She's probably rolling over in her grave somewhere." Bellamy's face fell for a moment, but she visibly shook herself. "Let's try these on."

Sarah sat outside the dressing room while Bellamy changed into a few of the dresses, modeling each one on the circular platform for Sarah to judge. She gave each one a score from 1 to 10, while the sales associates stood nearby, ooh-ing and ahh-ing at the appropriate times and fetching different sizes and styles for Bellamy to try.

Finally, Bellamy walked out and Sarah knew from the look on her face that this was the one. The sales associates had disappeared to the front of the store to help the only other customer, so it was up to Sarah to have the appropriate reaction.

It was an A-line gown with a heart-shaped lace bodice that fit Bellamy's slim waist perfectly. The bottom of the gown was pure white silk and it fell over her hips and to the floor like a waterfall. Intricate lace sleeves reached to Bellamy's wrists, tactfully covering the bandages on her arms.

Sarah held up her hands, fingers splayed, in a clear score. Ten out of ten.

Bellamy stepped up onto the platform and looked in the mirror. The smile on her face said more than words ever could.

This was the dress.

Raised voices echoed back to them from the front of the store. Sarah frowned and stood up, craning her neck to see what the commotion was. Someone was clearly super upset about their wedding dress.

She couldn't see over the racks of dresses, so she peeked down the aisle to where the cashier's station was.

Three black-clad men stood by the front, touting automatic rifles. "The money," one of them snarled at the cashier, a frightened teenage girl who didn't look any older than eighteen. He shoved the gun in her face, almost hitting her with it.

Oh crap.

Sarah pulled back, heart racing, and turned to Bellamy. "Get down," she whisper-shouted. "Get back in the dressing room and call 911."

Bellamy hopped off the platform, her expression tense. "What's going on?"

"Robbery." Sarah gestured toward the dressing room. "Hurry up. Go."

"I have my gun. It's in my purse. I'll just -"

"Bellamy." Sarah injected all the authority she could muster into her next words. "You're in no condition to confront armed robbers. Get in the dressing room, lock the door, and call the cavalry."

Bellamy hesitated for a heartbeat, then nodded once and disappeared. Sarah heard the soft "snick" of the lock engaging on the other side of the door and breathed a sigh of relief.

Crouching, she pulled her Glock out of its ankle holster. She kept her head low as she followed the row of wedding dresses around the store and toward the front.

Her heart pounded hard against her chest, but it wasn't

fear.

It was adrenaline.

This was her chance to prove she could hang with the big boys.

No way Emmett would turn her down after this.

"Where's the safe?" A male voice snapped. He had a bit of an accent, but he spoke too fast for Sarah to make out what it was.

She rose just high enough to peek over the tops of the dresses. The man had a gun to the cashier girl's head. She was shaking, tears streaming down her pretty face, mumbling that she didn't know where the safe was. Or that they didn't have one. Sarah was too far away to hear her exact words.

The other two men had disappeared, probably to fetch the getaway car. Perfect. One man was an easy target.

Sarah thumbed the safety on her Glock and shifted, ready to spring into action as soon as the opportunity presented itself.

A scream from the back of the store froze the blood in her veins.

The two missing men appeared, each holding an arm, and dragged Bellamy toward the register. Bellamy thrashed against them, cursing violently, but her dress was too long and she kept tripping over it.

Sarah's breath caught in her throat. Every cell in her body wanted to scream at them, threaten them not to hurt her or there would be hell to pay.

Instead, she held her position, every muscle primed to attack.

The three men talked fast to each other in a foreign language. It took Sarah a moment to recognize that it was Spanish. Her two years of Spanish in high school had nothing to offer her. They were speaking too fast for her to even make out individual words.

"The prize isn't here," one of them finally said in English. "Kill them and let's go."

Time slowed to a stop.

Bellamy's eyes widened. All the color drained from her face until she was as white as her wedding dress.

The wedding dress she would die in if Sarah didn't do something.

It was three against one. Her Glock against three automatic rifles.

She didn't stand a chance.

But no way was she going to watch another friend die.

Sarah released a breath and stood, aiming her gun at the man closest to Bellamy. Her first shot hit the man in the thigh. He went down, screaming obscenities in Spanish, and let go of Bellamy's arm.

Chaos broke out in the small store.

The three men yelled at each other, their voices mashing together into one jumble of panicked Spanish. The man holding Bellamy's other arm released her and grabbed his injured comrade. He fired a few times in Sarah's direction as he hauled the injured man toward the exit.

Sarah ducked, but he wasn't a good marksman. His spray of bullets went somewhere way over her head.

The last man took a few shots in her direction as well, but she had already disappeared into the clothing racks. She crouched, moving fast, and made her way to where Bellamy was struggling to her feet.

She saw the instant the robber made his decision. He couldn't find Sarah, so he aimed his gun at Bellamy.

Sarah didn't have a clear shot. She couldn't stop him.

She screamed a warning and dove for Bellamy, knocking them both sideways.

The gun went off, its blast loud in her ears.

Sarah landed on top of Bellamy. She rolled onto her knees and swung her gun up to fire before the man could get another shot off.

The sound of gunfire echoed in the store, but it wasn't Sarah's.

The man's shoulder jerked, spinning him to the right, and he went down.

Sarah staggered to her feet, gun still aimed at him, and glanced around.

Roman stood in the doorway with a gun in his hand, also pointed at the man on the ground. His chest rose and fell with rapid breaths and the expression on his face was terrifying.

Sirens blared in the distance.

"Sarah."

Bellamy's voice snapped Sarah out of her shock. She spun around and helped Bellamy into a seated position. Her face was still pale, her dark hair sticking up like she'd been struck by lightning.

Sarah's eyes swept her from head to toe, stuttering to a stop at the red stain on Bellamy's stomach. "Oh, God," she said. "You're hit."

"Sarah."

"Let me see it. We have to stop the bleeding, or-"

"Sarah!" Bellamy grabbed her hand. "It's not mine."

"What? But the blood..."

"I think it's yours."

"Huh?" Sarah looked down, dismayed, and touched a finger to the bloodstain spreading across her gray t-shirt. Oddly, she didn't feel any pain. "Oh."

"Sarah." Roman dropped to his knees next to her, his eyes on her side. "Let me see it."

Feeling suddenly weak, Sarah dropped to a sitting position. She reached down to pull up her shirt, but her hand was shaking so badly that she couldn't get a grip on the fabric.

"Don't touch it," Roman snapped. "Let me."

He pushed her hand out of the way and pulled up her shirt, baring her stomach. Blood oozed out of a wound at her side. She could tell at a glance that the bullet had passed through fatty tissue. Probably no organ damage. She reached around the back and found an exit wound.

As far as bullet wounds went, this was the best-case scenario.

She'd probably live to see another day.

"Do you have a first aid kit?" she called to the cashier. The girl stood frozen, watching them, her face as pale as Bellamy's. At Sarah's question, she nodded jerkily and ran toward the back of the store.

"You need to go to the hospital," Roman said. "You're hurt."

"No shit, Sherlock." Sarah narrowed her eyes at him.

"What are you doing here, anyway? It's getting freaky how often you show up where I am."

"I was in the area and heard gunshots." Roman held up his hand. It was covered in her blood. His expression darkened into a scowl. "I'm glad I was, or you might not be alive right now."

"I had it handled."

Roman opened his mouth to reply, but the police barreled into the store before he could piss Sarah off any more than he already had. An officer gestured for Roman to follow, saying something about taking a statement. Sarah wasn't really listening.

She put on a brave face, but the adrenaline was wearing off and the pain was setting in.

The cashier came back with a bright red pack. Sarah opened it and ripped open a package of gauze. Gritting her teeth, she forced her hands to remain steady and applied pressure to her wound.

Good thing Roman had his back to her, because judging from the stricken expression on Bellamy's face, Sarah's poker face had finally failed.

Did they have to blare those sirens so damn loud? Everyone in town could probably hear them. It was giving Sarah a headache.

The police had already cuffed the only man who hadn't escaped and hauled him away in a squad car. One officer taped off the area while others spoke to the employees.

Sarah tried to ignore the commotion around her and focus on wrapping an ace bandage around her waist. Once the gauze was secured to both bullet wounds, she allowed herself to take a breath. She'd done this a thousand times on the job, but it was a different matter to do it on herself.

Sarah glanced at Bellamy. She sat in the wedding gown, watching Sarah patch herself up. The color hadn't returned to her face yet. "I'm sorry I got blood all over your wedding dress," Sarah said.

Bellamy shook her head hard. "I'm just glad you're okay. I saw the blood and I thought..."

"I'll be fine." Sarah gestured at the bandage, forcing a smile. "See? Good as new."

"You still need to get to a hospital," Roman interrupted. He stepped up next to them, an officer on his heels, and held out a hand to help her up.

Sarah ignored him and pushed to her feet. The world turned on its axis and she staggered. Roman grabbed her shoulders to steady her. "Whoa. Thanks. Guess I lost more blood than I thought."

Roman muttered something under his breath. It sounded suspiciously like, "damned women."

Bellamy stood too, her expression concerned. "Are you sure you're okay?"

"Seriously. I'm fine."

"Do you need an ambulance?" The officer who'd distracted Roman asked.

"No, I'm taking her to the hospital now. You can get her statement later." Roman grasped Sarah's hand and started to lead her away, but she dug in her heels.

"I'm a big girl. I don't need you to boss me around."

Roman glowered at her. "You're coming with me, or I'll call Emmett."

Sarah locked gazes with him, willing him to concede defeat.

He didn't.

She sighed loudly. "Call Chance," she said to Bellamy. "Tell him you're okay. Then call Owen-"

"I got it." Bellamy nodded firmly. "We'll meet you at the hospital."

Sarah gave her a quick nod, then turned to follow Roman, already thinking of a thousand ways to rip him a new one in the car.

* * * * *

Roman opened the passenger door and waited impatiently for Sarah to get in. She tried to act tough, but she winced as she settled into the seat. Her hand pressed protectively against the bandage, which was already soaked in blood.

Roman slammed the door and stalked around to the driver's side. He caught sight of his blood-covered hand as he started the engine and clenched his jaw against a surge of rage.

That man was lucky to be alive. If Roman hadn't been so concerned about Sarah, he would have killed the asshole for hurting her.

The twenty-minute drive to the emergency room felt like an eternity.

"Why aren't you in Mexico with the team?" Sarah asked eventually. She looked at him with those inquisitive green eyes. Her blonde hair had fallen out of its ponytail. It framed her pale face, and damn it, she looked beautiful.

Roman tore his gaze away to watch the road. "Someone had to stay behind and keep an eye on the office."

He could tell she didn't believe him. She wasn't stupid.

The excuse wasn't any more believable than the one he'd used the night before.

He had "things" to take care of.

The truth was, Sarah *was* the thing he needed to take care of.

She'd been haunting his thoughts every day since she flounced into the ESI office, her blonde ponytail swinging, and demanded to join the team.

Since he'd lost his mind and kissed her in the hallway.

He didn't have time for distractions, and Sarah was a hell of a distraction.

Even worse, she was Ryan's roommate. The woman his brother had been in love with for years.

Roman's gut twisted with familiar grief. His little brother.

Dead at age 24.

Everything Roman had done to protect him...

In the end, it hadn't mattered.

Altez had found him and killed him anyway.

Roman pulled the truck into the hospital parking lot. Now was not the time for brooding about the past.

He went around to open the door for Sarah, but she'd already opened it and was struggling to get out.

Stubborn woman.

"Easy," Roman said, placing a hand under her elbow to steady her. "Can you walk?"

"Not really." She shot him a look. "But don't you dare even think about doing the macho thing and picking me up princess-style right now."

"Wouldn't dream of it."

He'd been thinking of doing just that.

Instead, he kept a hand at her elbow and walked at her pace into the emergency room. The nurses took one look at her and called for a stretcher.

"Well, thanks for the ride, I guess." Sarah's face contorted with pain as she gingerly laid flat. "And, you know, for saving my life."

Roman swallowed hard. "You're welcome."

"But let's not make this a thing. I had that situation under control."

He nodded. "Of course you did."

"Don't mock me." Sarah gave him the stink eye as the nurses wheeled her away. They called for a doctor as they disappeared through a set of double doors.

Roman stood there in the waiting room, uncertain of what he should do next. A nurse finally pointed him toward some chairs and he sat down, plopping his head into his hands.

The events of the robbery replayed in his mind, over and over again. The sound of gunfire. The vision of Sarah facing three armed men alone, her Glock raised defiantly.

Hell, she was a liar. She didn't have the situation handled.

She'd almost died.

The more he thought about it, the more sure he was that it wasn't a normal robbery.

Bradley's wasn't the most high-end store on that street. Wedding gowns were high-ticket items, but customers usually paid with a credit card. They wouldn't have much cash for the men to steal.

Why target Bradley's instead of somewhere else?

None of the men had been wearing masks, which implied that they didn't plan on leaving anyone alive to identify them after they were gone.

What was so valuable that they'd be willing to kill everyone in the store to get it?

The answer was obvious to him; Altez was behind it, and Sarah was the target. She had started digging, and Roman's worst fears had come to pass.

Altez knew about her.

Twenty minutes later, the doors flew open and Sarah's family came barreling in like a freight train with no brakes. Before they could harass the poor nurses, Roman waved them over.

"Where is she? Is she all right?" Sarah's mother demanded, wringing her hands.

"She's fine. I don't think she lost enough blood to need a transfusion. They're probably just cleaning the wound and stitching her up. She should be out soon."

"Thank God." Mary raised her hands, palms together, and rested her forehead on them in prayer.

Chance wrapped an arm around his mother's shoulders, but his eyes were on Bellamy. "We should get your stitches checked while we're here. I want to make sure you didn't pull anything when Sarah tackled you."

Bellamy shuddered. "I don't care if I did. If she hadn't

tackled me, I wouldn't be here right now."

Chance's jaw clenched. "If I could get my hands on those men..."

"... There wouldn't be anything left of them," Owen agreed.

Chance nodded, meeting Roman's eyes. "Thank you. The girls are lucky you were in the area."

Despite Chance's words, his gaze was sharp. Roman read the unspoken question loud and clear. Why wasn't he in Mexico with the team?

Luckily, Chance decided not to comment on it. Instead, he led Bellamy away to get checked out. Mary wandered off, muttering something about speaking to the doctor, leaving Roman and Owen alone.

Owen dropped into a chair and rubbed a hand over his face. His skin was pale, emphasizing the dark circles that were always under his eyes.

Roman sat down next to him, not sure what else to do. He wasn't part of the family, so it felt strange to wait here, but no way in hell he was leaving. He needed to make sure Sarah was really okay.

"Something doesn't feel right about this," Owen muttered after a few minutes.

Roman's head came up. "What do you mean?"

"I don't know. Never mind. I guess I'm just worried."

"She'll be fine. It was just a flesh wound."

"I hope so."

Roman frowned at the undertone in Owen's voice. Did he suspect something more than a mere robbery?

Had Sarah asked for his help looking for information on

Altez? If so, he was in danger too.

He'd been keeping an eye on the system at ESI and there hadn't been any pings to worry about. Could she have used another resource?

He wouldn't be surprised if she had. He was just barely starting to understand her tenacity.

If this robbery was more than a robbery...

Roman stood. "I'm going to see if I can have a word with that man in custody," he said, more to himself than to Owen.

Owen looked up. "Good idea. Care if I tag along?"

* * * * *

The phone rang, interrupting the quiet in Arturo's office.

He ignored it.

He had more important things to do than answer a petty phone call. The neighboring cartel was getting brave with their scouts; he'd captured two in the past week.

Antonio thought he could make a move on Arturo's territory.

What a fool.

Clearly he didn't understand the extent of Arturo's power and influence. He would have the U.S. government raiding Antonio's compound by the end of the week.

Antonio would be dead or captured before he ever thought of challenging Arturo again.

A knock sounded on his door, and Tomas poked his head in. "Altez," he said with a respectful bow. "I have news."

Arturo tamped down his irritation and waved the man in. "What is it?"

"I just received word from Manuel." Tomas paused and swallowed nervously. "They have failed, and Luis was captured."

Arturo snapped the pencil in his right hand. "The girl is still alive?"

"*Sí, señor.*"

"Tomas, I delegated this task to you. If there has been a misstep, I expect you to rectify it immediately."

Tomas shifted, clearly uncomfortable. "*Sí, señor.* I just thought you'd want to know."

Arturo fingered the handle on his desk drawer. His gun sat inside.

Tomas was annoying. Arturo had killed people for less.

But no. He needed the job done, and he didn't want to do it himself.

"The next time I hear from you, I expect good news. Do we understand each other?"

Tomas nodded emphatically and ducked out of the room before Arturo could change his mind.

Arturo threw the snapped pieces of his pencil in the trash and returned to the spreadsheets he'd been working on.

It was hard work to be the top crime lord in Mexico.

* * * * *

It was a silent ride to the police station.

Roman drove. He kept his eyes on the road, but his mind was imagining all the possible outcomes of that robbery.

Bellamy could've been killed.

Sarah could've been killed.

Altez had to be behind it. It was the only possible explanation.

But why was he going to so much trouble to kill Sarah? She was hardly a threat to him, even if she was digging.

Unless Altez knew about her connection to Roman.

But that was impossible. Roman had erased all evidence of himself. As far as the world knew, he was dead.

"Want to see a magic trick?"

Roman jerked out of his thoughts and glanced at Owen.

Owen held out a deck of cards. "Pick a card."

"You're seriously doing this right now?"

"It'll take your mind off things." Owen shook the cards at him. "Come on, you know you want to."

With a groan, Roman grabbed a card. It was the Queen of Hearts.

Fitting.

"All right, now slide it back into the deck. Anywhere's fine." Owen watched as Roman slid it back into the middle. "Good. Now watch."

He shuffled the deck a few times, humming to himself. Then he threw it into the air. Cards scattered across the interior of Roman's truck.

Still humming, Owen plucked a card that had stuck to the inside of the windshield and showed it to Roman. "Is this your card?"

It was the Queen of Hearts.

Roman stifled a smile. "How did you do that?"

"Magic. Duh." Owen grinned. "You saved my sister's life today, you know."

"I didn't do much. Sarah did most of the work herself."

"She's a strong woman." Owen started gathering the cards scattered over the seat. "But not as strong as she thinks she is sometimes."

"I've noticed."

"She has a tendency to get in over her head."

"Yes, she does."

Owen eyed him, sliding the now-intact deck of cards back into his pocket. "I have a feeling you know more about her weird behavior lately than you're letting on."

He was an intuitive one.

Roman was careful to keep his expression neutral.

"Sure, you don't have to tell me. I'm just glad she has someone watching her back. She needs it."

Owen settled back into his seat, humming, and turned his gaze out the window.

Roman swallowed hard.

If Sarah was on Altez's radar, she'd need all the help she could get.

Roman just hoped he was enough.

* * * * *

"Sarah! What are you doing? Why aren't you in bed?"

Sarah rolled her eyes and gingerly lowered herself into a chair at the kitchen table. "I'm fine, Mom. It's just a scratch."

"Just a...?" Mary looked flabbergasted. "You were shot. The doctor said not to move around too much or you'll pull your stitches."

"I'm being careful." Sarah grabbed a piece of bread off the platter in the middle of the table and took a bite.

Mary huffed, but turned back to the stove. She knew Sarah well enough to know that arguing was pointless. The house phone rang, and she wiped her hands on her apron before she picked it up.

"Erickson residence." Her voice softened. "Hi, baby."

Sarah grabbed another piece of bread.

Mary paused, listening, and glanced over her shoulder at Sarah. "I see. All right, I'll tell her. Love you too."

"What is it?"

Mary returned the phone to the receiver. "Chance just got a call from the police station. The man involved in the robbery, the one they caught... He escaped."

"What?" All that bread Sarah ate threatened to come back up. "How did he escape police custody?"

"I don't know, honey. Chance didn't say."

The room spun. Sarah gripped the edge of the table so she wouldn't fall over.

"They're making efforts to look for him," Mary was saying. Her voice sounded like it was coming from the end of a long tunnel. "He was injured, so they don't think he got far. I'm sure they'll find him."

Sarah pushed away from the table and stood, gritting her teeth against the queasiness. "I'm going to go for a drive."

"You're injured." Mary waved a wooden spoon at her. "What part of the doctor's orders did you not understand?"

"The part where I have to sit on my hands at home." Sarah grabbed her keys off the kitchen counter. "Sorry, Mom. I'll be back in a bit."

Mary looked like she wanted to protest further, but Sarah brushed a kiss across her cheek and walked quickly out the front door before she could get out a full sentence.

Sarah drove for a while. She didn't know where she was going, but anywhere was better than the house. The walls felt like they were closing in on her, and she'd only been there a few hours since she was discharged from the hospital.

Sarah winced at the twinge in her side.

She could've died.

The thought hit her like a punch to the gut. She hadn't let the events of the day sink in yet, nor did she want to. She didn't want to consider what could have happened if she'd been half a second slower.

Bellamy could've been shot instead of her.

She definitely didn't want to think about what could've happened if Roman hadn't shown up. Maybe she wouldn't have been able to get off another shot before the man killed her.

Roman. Why had he been there?

His story about keeping an eye on the office was bull, and she knew it. He'd been dressed in tactical gear like the rest of them when she ran into him outside the bathroom. Why did he stay home?

Was it because of her?

Sarah snorted. Of course not. He didn't care about anyone but himself.

But the gentleness she'd seen at the hospital was real. She could still feel his hand on her elbow, helping her inside, its warmth spreading through her whole body.

Before Sarah knew it, she was parked in front of the ESI office. The lights were on despite the late hour. Who could possibly be working this late?

She ignored the part of her that hoped it was Roman.

The front door was locked, but Sarah had stolen Owen's code weeks ago. She punched it in and smiled as she pushed the door open.

The lounge was empty, so Sarah followed the light down the hallway.

It led her to Owen's office. He sat in front of his wall of monitors, leaned back in his chair, with his feet on the desk. With one hand, he shuffled a deck of playing cards. The other rested on the mouse in his lap, moving his cursor across the screen. He muttered irritably under his breath.

"What's going on?"

Owen jumped. Playing cards shot across the room as he spun around to glare at her. "Jeez! Do you get off on scaring the hell out of me?" His eyes narrowed. "Why aren't you resting?"

Sarah shrugged. "I wanted out of the house. What are you doing?"

Owen sighed and turned back to the monitors. He'd given up trying to tell her what to do a long time ago. "I'm just looking at the latest images from Emmett and the team. It doesn't look good."

Sarah stepped up next to him and squinted at the screens. "Why? What happened?"

"Nothing happened. This cartel is extremely well-equipped. Look at this." He pointed at the aerial photo of what looked like a small village. A thick cement wall surrounded the cluster of buildings, with four circles in each corner of the perimeter.

"What are those?" she asked, pointing at them.

"Guard towers. Armed with two guards each and a mounted machine gun."

Sarah let out a low whistle. "How did they get that picture? Did you hack a satellite?"

"Drone. Remote controlled, armed with the latest camouflage technology."

"Wow. That's cool."

Owen snorted. "That's not even the coolest thing we've got. Uncle Sam gives us cool toys when we do the dirty work for him. But that's not the point. This cartel is dangerous. No wonder the government sent us in first to check it out. If they'd sent a team to infiltrate, it would've been a massacre."

"Are Emmett and the others in danger?"

He shrugged. "They're always in danger, but they're in stealth mode, so right now it's minimal."

If Emmett wasn't such a jerk, Sarah could be helping with assignments like this. Her small frame would be useful for sneaking around.

She wasn't giving up. Emmett would accept her onto the team, whether he liked it or not.

"When are they coming back?"

"The last transmission from Emmett said they were just finishing up and heading back to the plane. They should be here by tomorrow morning."

"Have you told him about what happened?"

Owen shook his head. "Not while he's on mission. Distractions can lead to death in the field."

"Oh, right." Sarah studied the other photos of the compound. "So why did the government want you to check this out?"

"Could be a number of reasons. They might be planning a raid, or it could be for informational purposes. They weren't very forthcoming. They wouldn't even tell us any information about the cartel that owns this place."

"That seems sketchy."

"It is. But they pay good money, so we do as we're told."

* * * * *

The lounge wasn't empty when Sarah left. Roman sprawled in a lounge chair in the corner. He looked up when she left Owen's office and his eyes followed her down the hallway and into the lobby.

"Why aren't you resting?"

Sarah rolled her eyes. "If one more person asks me that, I'm going to shoot myself in the head."

"It's a valid question. You were shot, you know."

"I'm aware."

Roman stood and crossed the room in a few strides. He was dressed in dark jeans and a black t-shirt. As usual, his scar made him look menacing. "You should be in bed."

Sarah felt her cheeks warm under his perusal. "Don't worry about me. I can take care of myself."

"It seems you have a tendency to get yourself into trouble."

She took a step back. Why did he always have to stand in her personal space? "Maybe I do. Keeps things interesting."

"That's what I'm afraid of." His eyes were dark, almost black in the dim light.

Her stomach did a weird flip. "W-Well, like you said, it's been an eventful day. Getting shot and all. Guess I'll head home to bed."

Sarah ducked past him. She felt hot all over and she didn't like it.

"Goodnight," he called after her.

His words sent goosebumps across her skin. Sarah waved a hand over her shoulder, but she didn't look back. She didn't want him to see how red her face was.

CHAPTER 7

THE NEXT MORNING, Sarah woke to a text from Tom.
I found something. Can we meet this afternoon?
Sure. What time?
3:00 @ that coffee shop we used to go to.

Sarah put her phone down, excitement brimming in her chest. It must be important for him to request a meeting in person. Maybe he found something that would finally send her in the right direction.

She spent the morning lounging on the couch under her mother's watchful eye, watching re-runs of Friends. She was sore, but the pain wasn't terrible enough to warrant bedrest. But Mary looked so dismayed the night before that Sarah complied with her request.

At 2:30, Sarah made her excuses and left the house. Her plan worked; her mother didn't argue with her.

Probably because she thought Sarah was going to a doctor's appointment.

Sarah climbed into her Jeep and started driving toward downtown.

She was only driving for a few minutes when she noticed the black truck following her.

The area around her parents' house was pretty unpopulated, and she knew all the cars on the road.

This wasn't one of her neighbor's cars.

But it also wasn't a bad guy.

She'd bet money that it was Roman's truck.

He *was* following her.

Sarah's blood boiled.

Did nobody think she was capable of taking care of herself? She didn't need a bodyguard following her around all day.

And she certainly didn't want a shadow during her meeting with Tom.

Sarah performed three right turns just to be sure.

Sure enough, the black truck made the same maneuvers.

"All right, Roman," she muttered. "Let's dance."

She turned onto the more populated highway as if she was heading out of town and sped up to blend into the flow of traffic.

Roman remained a few cars behind her.

After a few minutes, she turned off the main road and stopped in the left turn lane at a light. Cars stacked up on the opposite side.

There was no green arrow on this light, so she would be stuck there for a few minutes until an opportunity to turn would appear.

Roman's truck pulled in behind her.

Sarah rolled down her window and stuck her fist

outside the Jeep. She gave Roman the middle-finger salute.

She saw the flash of his teeth in her rearview mirror.

The light turned green.

Time to shoot the gap.

Sarah floored it. The Jeep screamed into the intersection. Several angry cars honked their horns as she flew past them, but she made the left turn before any of them could hit her.

Roman's truck moved forward as if it would do the same, but cars already started streaming through the intersection.

Sarah laughed out loud. "Who says I'm not skilled enough to join ESI?"

She took a circuitous route back to downtown La Conner, careful to make a series of turns that made no sense.

Roman never caught back up to her.

The coffee shop Tom had mentioned was a hole-in-the-wall joint they frequented in high school. They sold cheap bagels and free coffee with every purchase. Miraculously, they were still in business.

The smell of bread dough brought back memories as Sarah stepped inside the shop. It looked the same as it had in high school, albeit a little more run-down. Grimy tan tile covered the floors and turquoise wallpaper peeled from the walls.

Sarah settled into a chair at three o'clock on the dot and waited.

And waited. And waited.

She called Tom's cell, but it went straight to voicemail.

An hour into her wait, she called the police station.

The cranky receptionist answered the phone.

"Hi, is Tom there? This is Sarah Erickson."

"No." She still sounded bored. La Conner was a quiet town, aside from the random burglary yesterday, so she probably didn't see much excitement. "He left a few hours ago. Have you tried his cell?"

"Yeah I did. Thanks anyway."

Sarah waited a few more minutes, growing more anxious by the second. Had he forgotten about their meeting? Maybe he'd gotten busy with something.

Or maybe…

She looked through her address book and found his wife Jennifer's phone number.

"Hello?"

"Hi… Jennifer?"

"Yes, who is this?"

"Sorry, this is Sarah Erickson. I'm an old friend of Tom's."

"Oh, hi." Jennifer's voice was warm. Sarah had only met her once, at their wedding a few years ago, but obviously she remembered her. "How are you?"

"I'm great, thanks. Have you seen Tom? Is he with you?"

"No, I've been at work all day. I won't be home until later tonight. Why?"

Sarah frowned. Goosebumps prickled across her skin. "He was supposed to meet me for coffee but he never showed. That's not like him, so I got worried."

Jennifer laughed. "He's been pretty forgetful lately. He probably just went home without remembering he was supposed to meet you."

"Okay, thanks. Maybe I'll check there."

It didn't take long to find Tom's house. It was a cute two-story building on the edge of town, with a small porch and red shutters. The lawn was well-manicured and Tom's car sat in the driveway.

Sarah breathed a sigh of relief as she parked behind it. Maybe he just forgot about her after all.

She knocked on the front door and waited. No answer.

Frowning, she put her ear to the door and listened. She couldn't hear any noises inside. Biting her lip, she tried the doorknob and was surprised when it turned. Unlocked.

That wasn't like Tom.

Sarah pushed the door open and peered inside. "Tom?" she called. "It's Sarah. Are you here?"

No answer.

Something wasn't right. Sarah pulled her Glock from its holster - was this really the second time she was drawing it in two days?

She checked the bottom floor, but she didn't find anyone, so she climbed the stairs to the upper floor. The stairs led to a hallway. All the doors were closed except one, which was cracked, and spilled light onto the carpet.

"Tom?" Sarah nudged the door open, her grip tight on her Glock, and peeked into a bedroom. Her gaze roamed over the bed and dresser until it landed on two feet sticking out past the end of the bed on the opposite side.

"Tom!"

Sarah rushed forward and fell to her knees beside Tom's body, her Glock falling forgotten at her side. His eyes were closed. A prescription bottle lay open on the carpet next to his hand.

An *empty* prescription bottle.

No, no, no.

Sarah felt for a pulse at his wrist. Nothing.

She tried his neck.

Put her ear against his chest.

"Oh my God," she sobbed. With shaking hands, she pulled out her cell phone and dialed 911. She put it on speaker and dropped it on the floor next to Tom's head. Then she kneeled over his body and began CPR.

"Please don't die on me," she begged between compressions. "Please, not you too. Come on. Wake up!"

Her mind couldn't process what her heart had already realized.

Tom was dead.

* * * * *

Sarah was familiar with the steps of processing a dead body.

But far too often lately, they were bodies of people she loved.

She continued CPR until the police and an ambulance arrived. After they asked her a few preliminary questions, she was pushed to the side and the EMTs did their work. It didn't take them long to pronounce Tom dead at the scene.

Sarah waited in a daze while the officers cordoned off the area and began taking pictures of Tom and the surrounding evidence. The coroner arrived and she watched as Tom's body was taken away, probably to the morgue where Jennifer would be called in to identify him.

As they carried Tom's body out of the room in a black body bag, Sarah ran to the bathroom and threw up.

Several hours later, after she had been sufficiently questioned by the authorities and helped Jennifer ID the body, Sarah sat on the front steps of the police station with her head in her hands. Jennifer's expression when they pulled back the white sheet would haunt Sarah until the day she died.

Sarah closed her eyes and rubbed gentle circles at her temples. She could probably sleep for a week and still be exhausted, but the CPR had pulled on her stitches. Her side throbbed in time with the pain she felt in her chest.

Footsteps approached her, but she didn't lift her head or open her eyes until she heard someone drop onto the step next to her.

"Heard you had a rough day today."

Was she relieved or annoyed to hear Roman's voice? She wasn't sure. Probably more annoyed. "Let me guess... it's a coincidence that you're here?"

"Exactly. I happened to be walking by and I saw you sitting here. Trouble seems to follow you wherever you go, so it seemed like a good idea to stay nearby." Roman's tone was light, as if he was gauging her emotional state.

Her emotional state was not good. Not good at all.

"What happened?" His voice was gentle, like he was talking to a wounded animal.

It pissed Sarah off. She didn't deserve kindness, not today.

"One of my oldest friends committed suicide," she said flatly. She looked up at him, hoping her stare was as cold as she felt on the inside. "Only it wasn't suicide. Just like Ryan's mugging wasn't a mugging."

Roman's expression went from gentle to hard as a rock, faster than she could re-think the wisdom of her words. "I told you to leave that alone."

Sarah didn't reply. Connections were forming in her mind, now that the shock had begun to fade. No, Tom's death wasn't a coincidence.

It was her fault.

She was going to be sick again.

"Sarah," Roman prompted. She met his eyes, and her expression must've revealed what she was thinking. "You didn't leave it alone, did you?"

Sarah stood. She took a few deep breaths, counting to twenty in her head so she wouldn't freak out. She'd asked Tom to look into Altez because she had too much pride to ask her brothers for help.

Now Tom was dead.

Whatever he'd found had gotten him killed.

Whoever this Altez guy was, he was far more powerful than she could've imagined.

"Sarah." Roman stood too. He grabbed her shoulders and gave her a small shake. "Why can't you let this go?"

She looked into his eyes. It wasn't annoyance she saw there, or lack of caring. Roman was frustrated, yes, but he also looked... scared. "You do know something," she whispered.

Roman's eyes narrowed. "What did you do?"

He knew. He'd known something all along.

Sarah took a step back. Her mind was reeling. She needed somewhere to sit and think, to work through everything that was happening.

Roman looked like he wanted to grab her again, but she shook her head and backed up another step.

"Whatever you know, I don't want to hear it right now." She turned and began to walk away, back to her Jeep.

"Sarah." Roman caught up to her easily. His long strides matched hers as he fell into step beside her. "Tell me what's going on."

"What's going on? I have now watched two of my best friends die right in front of me." Sarah quickened her pace. "And I'm sure as hell not going to let it happen again. Butt out, Roman. You didn't want to be involved in the first place."

"You don't know what you're dealing with-"

They reached her Jeep. Sarah slid into the driver's seat and slammed the door. Her stitches pulled, but she didn't care. She rolled down her window and looked Roman square in the eye.

"Bite me."

Then she hit the gas and squealed away, leaving him standing on the curb.

* * * * *

Later that night, Sarah sat cross-legged on the floor of

her childhood bedroom, staring at her still-packed suitcase. It was late; the house was quiet except for the sound of her own heart racing in her ears.

She drew her knees into her chest and wrapped her arms around them. What should she do now?

Her only lead to Altez was dead. Jennifer's pale, distraught face flashed in her mind again. The words she'd whispered to Sarah after they identified Tom's body.

"I'm pregnant. I was going to tell him tonight."

He'd never find out if he was having a boy or girl, and it was Sarah's fault. He would never be able to sing lullabies to his daughter or teach his son to swing a baseball bat. One favor for an old friend had robbed an unborn child of the chance to know his or her father.

Sarah swallowed the bile rising in her throat and took a deep breath. She could continue to wallow in self-pity, or she could do something productive.

She unzipped her suitcase and flipped it open. Methodically, she began unpacking and folding her clothes into neat piles on the floor around her. When she picked up a shirt, she caught her breath when she saw the pile of Ryan's things underneath. In all the craziness, she'd forgotten that she'd taken them from his bedroom when she was cleaning everything out.

Sarah pulled out his DSLR camera and smiled faintly. She turned it over in her hands, running her fingers over the scuffed case. The buttons were so well-worn that the small labels had completely rubbed away. Ryan never went anywhere without that camera around his neck.

Wait a minute.

She thought back to the last few days before Ryan was killed. He'd been distracted, disappearing for hours at a time. When Sarah tried to ask him where he was going all the time, he'd smiled secretly. *"Wouldn't you like to know?"*

He brought home Chinese food the week before he died. They watched The Big Bang Theory on TV and ate greasy orange chicken and Ryan took pictures of Sarah trying to use her chopsticks. She warned him that if he didn't delete them, she would make sure his camera didn't live to see another day.

He'd just smiled and took a picture of them together, in their pajamas, grinning with their chopsticks in hand.

Sarah desperately hoped he'd ignored her demand. She flipped the power switch and the small LED screen lit up. She hit the button to review old pictures. A black screen appeared, with white lettering across the middle.

File Corrupted.

Of course. Fate had even stolen the chance to see the last photos that Ryan ever took.

That's right; this was the SD card Jose was looking for that night.

It should have the answers Sarah was looking for, but it didn't.

Sarah set the camera on her bed and turned to look at the remaining treasures in her suitcase. She pulled out a stack of photos that had littered Ryan's desk. Pictures of her at the park when they dog-sat their professor's boxer for a week. A picture of her doing the dishes, singing along to the radio. A picture of Ryan at the coffee shop where they always studied, his medical textbook in front of him. Sarah was asleep on her textbook next to him and Ryan was grinning from ear to ear, holding another book high in the air.

Sarah remembered that day. He had slammed the book down on the desk and it had scared her so badly that she didn't talk to him for the rest of the day.

Tears slipped down Sarah's cheeks. She examined each photo carefully, envisioning each memory as though it was happening right at that moment.

Sometime during the night, she fell asleep like that, curled up on the floor with Ryan's photos scattered around her.

CHAPTER 8

THE SMELL OF HER MOTHER'S FRENCH TOAST drew Sarah downstairs the next morning. She staggered into the kitchen with bleary, red-rimmed eyes and mussed hair. Judging from the raised eyebrows her mother gave her, Sarah looked as terrible as she felt.

"Good morning!" Mary's voice was overly cheerful as she set a steaming plate of food in front of her. "How are you feeling, honey?"

"Peachy," Sarah mumbled, shoving a forkful of food in her mouth.

"How are your stitches? Want me to take a look at them?"

"Already did. They're fine."

Her mother hesitated for a moment like she wanted to say something more, but instead she turned back to the stove and the next batch of French toast, leaving Sarah to her thoughts.

Sarah was almost done with breakfast when the front door burst open. The sound of deep, raised voices carried into the kitchen. With a groan, Sarah pushed her plate away and steeled herself.

"Sarah!" Emmett stomped into the kitchen. He glowered at her where she sat, his eyes sweeping from her face, down to her side, then back up again. "What the hell happened?"

Blustering was how Emmett showed his concern. Sarah had been on the receiving end of it so many times that she wasn't impressed by his scare tactics.

"I'm sure you've already heard the details from Owen," she said calmly, shooting Owen a you-better-have-given-the-best-version-possible look over Emmett's shoulder. "Everyone's fine. We were just in the wrong place at the wrong time."

Emmett narrowed his eyes. "Chance told me you saved Bellamy's life."

"Guess I wouldn't be so useless as an ESI agent after all."

He crossed his arms over his chest and scowled. "One robbery doesn't make you fit for the field, and the fact that you don't know that is proof enough that you're not ready to join the team."

Sarah mentally counted to ten. When she still wanted to rip Emmett's head off, she went ahead and continued to twenty.

"I think I've proven that I can handle myself," she finally said. "So you can call off your guard dog."

"What?"

"Come on, Emmett. I'm not twelve years old, and I don't need Roman following me around to make sure I'm safe."

Emmett's frown deepened. "I don't know what you're talking about. Roman has been following you?"

So it wasn't an assignment. Roman had been tailing her for his own reasons.

Interesting.

"Never mind. Forget it."

Emmett let the subject drop. "I heard about Tom."

Sarah stiffened and stood up, almost knocking her chair over in her haste. "Yeah, I don't really want to talk about it."

Dropping her plate in the sink, she fled the kitchen before her calm veneer shattered. She half expected Emmett to follow her and continue his interrogation, but it wasn't him that leaned beside her on the deck railing a few moments later.

It was Owen.

"What's going on with you?"

"It's been a long few weeks. I think I'm entitled to feel a little out of sorts."

"Drop the act," he said impatiently. "Twin psychic powers aside, I know you better than anyone else. You've been acting weird ever since you came home. You asked me to find that name for you and refused to give me any information about it. Then your friend at the police station turned up dead. What have you gotten yourself into?"

"Nothing, Owen."

"Are you telling me it's a coincidence?"

"It is."

"Bullshit."

Sarah's spine stiffened. Owen didn't usually curse; he was genuinely frustrated with her. But what could she say that would satisfy him without getting him involved? She couldn't afford to bring anyone else in on this... not after what happened to Tom.

"Whatever's going on, let me help you. Why are you keeping secrets from me?"

She bit her lip. She wanted so badly to tell him, to share the colossal weight that had settled on her shoulders since Ryan's death. Looking into his eyes, she allowed him to see the emotions she'd been hiding. The pain, desperation, guilt, and grief that were swallowing her.

"I know you don't understand," she whispered. "But please... just keep this between us, okay? I'm not ready to talk about things yet."

"You don't have to talk about anything. Just tell me what I can do to help."

Sarah shook her head. "I can't, Owen. Not right now."

She couldn't lose anyone else she cared about, especially Owen.

He looked at her a moment longer. A muscle worked in his jaw.

Finally, he turned and walked away, leaving Sarah alone on the deck with her guilt.

She sighed, looking out at the trees beyond the backyard. It killed her to lie to her family, especially Owen, but there was no other option. If she told him everything now, he would immediately go to Emmett and the whole family would get involved.

Emmett, who risked his life on a daily basis with ESI. He

cared more deeply about people than he would ever admit. If he knew the truth, he wouldn't rest until he found this Altez person and either captured or killed him.

Owen, who knew her better than anyone else. He could sense how much pain she was in and he wanted to fix it.

Chance, who just recently went through hell to bring Bellamy back into his life. He should be joyously planning a wedding, not helping her avenge Ryan's death.

Oh, God.

Bellamy. She'd asked Bellamy for help.

If Tom was killed for searching Altez's name, was Bellamy in danger too?

Sarah fumbled with her pocket and pulled out her cell phone.

Bellamy answered on the first ring. "Hey, is everything okay?"

"Bellamy." Sarah didn't even try to hide the panic in her voice. "Do you remember that name I asked you to look up?"

"Yeah, I'm still waiting to hear back from – "

"Forget it."

"What?"

"I said forget it. I don't need to know. I don't want to know."

"Sarah, what's going on?"

Sarah took a deep breath. "As my best friend, I'm asking you to listen to me without asking questions."

"... Okay."

"I should never have asked you to look up that name.

Drop it and leave it alone, okay?"

"All right, if you say so, but – "

"I can't explain right now." Sarah gripped the deck railing with her other hand, so tight that her knuckles turned white. "Just do me a favor and watch your back."

Ominous silence filled the line. "You sure you don't want me to tell Chance? ESI can probably help."

"No, not right now. I'll let you know if that changes."

"Okay." Bellamy hesitated. "For the record, this goes against my better judgment. But I'll stay quiet."

"Thanks. I'll talk to you later."

Sarah hung up and released a breath. She leaned forward until her forehead touched the railing.

Hopefully Bellamy listened to her and let it go.

Sarah needed to handle this on her own.

She thought of Ryan and Tom. Ryan, who had such a bright future ahead of him as a doctor. Tom, who never knew he had a son or daughter waiting to meet him.

But it wasn't just because she owed it to Ryan and Tom.

She owed it to herself.

She needed to prove to herself that she had the power to take care of her own affairs. Maybe it was because Emmett thought she wasn't good enough to join ESI. Maybe it was because she'd felt helpless too often recently.

Sarah shook her head and pushed away from the railing.

She would find Altez and make him pay for what he'd taken.

From Roman. From Jen.

From her.

* * * * *

Bellamy ended the call and dropped her cell phone on the bed, frowning.

"What's wrong?" Chance asked, entering their bedroom.

Bellamy was momentarily distracted by his bare chest and the towel wrapped around his hips. "Uh, what?"

Chance noticed her distraction and smiled slyly. "Who was on the phone?"

"Just Sarah. She wanted to make sure I was doing okay." Bellamy's eyes followed him as he went to the dresser and pulled out a pair of clean boxers.

Chance looked over his shoulder at her. "Is that all?"

Bellamy hesitated when Chance dropped the towel and she was gifted with a glimpse of his bare bum while he pulled on his boxers.

When she didn't answer, Chance turned around and cocked an eyebrow at her.

"Uh, what were we talking about?" Bellamy reached for Chance's hand and pulled him toward her. "You know what, it doesn't matter."

CHAPTER 9

SARAH RAN DOWN A LONG, NARROW HALLWAY. A dark figure stood at the end, facing away from her.

It was Altez; she knew it was.

But no matter how fast and how hard she ran, he seemed to shrink further out of her reach.

His mocking laughter rang in her ears.

She screamed insults, pleaded with him to turn around. Finally, he did.

But there was a yawning black hole where his face was supposed to be, a swirling blackness that sucked her in.

She screamed, but no one could hear her.

She was alone--

The slight creak of her wood floor brought Sarah instantly awake. She caught a glimpse of a real-life dark figure leaning over her bed an instant before something big and cold covered her face.

She tried to scream, but the sound was too muffled for anyone to hear.

It was a pillow. This guy - it had to be a man - was

smothering her with her own pillow.

She couldn't take a breath. She couldn't breathe.

Sarah tried to scramble away from him, but his weight kept her pinned in place. Her fists battered uselessly against his body.

Her strength was failing. She felt consciousness begin to slip away.

Her gun. She kept it on her nightstand.

It was dark; maybe the man hadn't seen it. If she could only reach...

Her fingers closed around something hard. It wasn't her gun, but it was a heavy, oval hand mirror that her mother had bought her at an antique shop when she was a teenager.

Sarah swung the mirror in the general direction of her attacker's head. Her blow didn't have the power it normally would, but it hit hard.

It was enough to shift his weight slightly off her.

Sarah swung her legs up and underneath the man's - yes, definitely a man's - chest and pushed with the last of her strength. Her stitches screamed at the pressure and she felt at least one of them pop out, but she was free.

She heard a gratuitous thump as the man's body hit the floor.

Sarah shoved the pillow away and sucked in a deep breath of wonderful, delicious air.

The man rose again; she could barely make out his form in the pitch-black room.

This time, when Sarah screamed, she made sure it was loud enough to wake the whole house. She dove across the room at the man. His movement faltered as if he wasn't expecting her to have so much strength left.

She tackled him and they both hit the ground, rolling into her desk. There was a loud clatter as her line of trophies toppled to the floor.

"Who are you?" Sarah said, out of breath.

The man threw a punch. Sarah tried to dodge, but her reflexes were too slow. It clipped her eye and she let out a furious yell. She blocked his next swing with her forearm and kneed him in the groin. The man doubled over with a pained grunt.

Sarah bared her teeth in a satisfied smile.

Her bedroom door flew open. Owen was illuminated in the light from the hallway. He was shirtless, his hair sticking up on one side, but he looked alert and coldly furious. His gun was trained on her attacker's chest.

"Sarah, get away from him."

Sarah scrambled to her feet, breathing hard, and aimed one more kick at the man's stomach before she stepped back. Now that she wasn't in immediate danger, the pain radiating from her side drew her attention. She pressed a hand to the area and grimaced when her palm came away wet with blood.

Owen approached the attacker, gun steady. "Call the police."

While Sarah dialed 911, she stood next to Owen and stared down at the man. He had gone completely still and his hands were up in a gesture of surrender.

Sarah stepped forward and yanked the black ski mask off his head.

It was one of the men from the robbery, the one who had left early with the man she'd shot in the leg.

"Who are you?" she demanded for the second time. "What do you want with me?"

The man glared obtusely at them and muttered a string of Spanish she couldn't understand.

"Do you recognize him?" Owen asked.

Sarah stood and stepped back. "Yeah," she said finally as reality began to sink in. "I do."

* * * * *

Three times in one week had to be some kind of record.

Sarah slouched in a chair at the police station, scowling at the officers who huddled around a desk on the other side of the room. Owen had dropped her off after the police arrested her mystery attacker so she could give her statement.

He hadn't bothered to stick around. Apparently, he had "things to take care of."

Those "things" probably consisted of hacking the police and national database to figure out who the bozo was.

And also alerting Emmett to the situation.

He stormed into the police station about an hour later. His gaze was murderous.

A common expression lately where she was concerned.

He stopped in front of her first and glared down at her. "What the hell is going on?"

Sarah stood gingerly, a hand still at her side. She'd looked at her wound before they left the house and, sure enough, she'd torn two of her stitches in her fight with the mystery man. It was bleeding and it hurt like a bitch, but she'd covered it with gauze and an ace bandage until she could make it back to the hospital.

"I want to listen to the interrogation," she told Emmett quietly, aware of the officers staring at them.

Emmett continued to glare at her, a silent command for her to answer his question.

She stared back, broadcasting loud and clear that she wouldn't say a word until her demand was met.

Emmett's brows lowered and he stalked off to the huddled policemen. She couldn't make out what he said, just the commanding tone of his voice.

Because ESI had helped in a lot of local cases, Emmett had some major clout where the police were concerned. She was counting on that to get her into that interrogation observation room.

It took a few minutes, but finally Emmett looked over his shoulder and gestured for her to approach. Sarah followed him and another officer, studiously keeping her gaze away from Tom's office, which they passed on their way to the interrogation room.

The officer let them in. Another man, dressed in plainclothes, stood on the other side of the room. He must have been an investigator on the case, but Sarah didn't recognize him. He and Emmett exchanged respectful nods, then they all turned their attention to the large window that looked into the interrogation room.

Her attacker slouched in a chair on one side of a metal table, facing the two-way mirror. His hands were cuffed together and his fingers tapped rhythmically on the table's surface.

1, 2, 3, 4. ·

1, 2, 3, 4.

"Mister Montoya," another man - the lead investigator, probably - said. "You were caught in that young lady's room. Not only is that trespassing, but I can book you for assault and attempted murder. The only logical thing to do here is to tell me who you're working for so I can help you."

Montoya looked bored. He eyed the investigator and didn't answer.

His fingers kept tap-tapping on the metal surface.

The investigator paced around the table, looking completely unruffled.

It was impressive that he was able to remain calm. Sarah wanted to climb through that window and strangle Montoya herself.

"I did some digging on you, you know," the investigator said casually. "I know you came to America last year, and you have your mother and sister with you."

Montoya stiffened.

"What's the fee these days to cross the border illegally, I wonder? I couldn't find any paperwork on your mother or your sister. Only for you. That's odd, isn't it?"

Sweat appeared on Montoya's forehead, shining in the fluorescent light. His fingers began to tap their rhythm faster and faster.

"I wonder what the government would do if someone, say, reported some illegal immigrants living here. There are far fewer opportunities in Mexico, I hear."

Montoya's face contorted in anger. He leaned forward. "Leave my ma and sister out of this," he spat. His voice was thick with a Hispanic accent.

The investigator placed both palms on the table. "Then tell me who hired you."

"I can't."

"Then I can't help your mother and sister."

Montoya leaned back. His expression flashed from anger to fear and back in an instant. "He'll kill me."

"The government can protect you, Mister Montoya. Nobody will be able to harm you here. But you have to help us before we can do that. That's the way it works."

Montoya looked at him for a long time, weighing his options. "I want to speak to her," he said finally. "The girl. I want to speak to her."

Sarah's blood turned to ice. Emmett glanced down at her. The "hell no" was so obvious in his expression that he might as well have screamed it.

The investigator slipped out of the room through a side door and then entered the observation room. He nodded at the three of them and his eyes found Sarah. "You heard him. It's against protocol, but" - he glanced at Emmett - "we could make an exception this time."

Sarah bit her lip and looked at Montoya.

He'd almost killed her tonight. She'd almost ended up just like Ryan and Tom.

But he wasn't the boogeyman she was really after.

If this was the only way to get him to talk, she didn't really have a choice. She needed something more substantial to go on if she was going to find Altez.

Sarah gave a curt nod to the investigator. He bobbed his head in response and opened the door for her.

Before she could move, Emmett grabbed her elbow. "I don't like this."

"Tough cookies." Sarah shook him off and followed the investigator.

It was odd to stare into the face of the man who had almost killed her.

Sarah tried to remain calm as she sat down in the chair across from him. She looked like the victim everyone probably thought she was. Her shirt was soaked with blood from her wound and her right eye was swollen shut and rapidly turning dark purple.

"Here I am." She was impressed with how steady her voice sounded. "Say what you have to say."

Montoya looked her up and down, examining her as if seeing her for the first time. It probably was, because he'd previously only seen her ducking behind clothing racks and sleeping in the darkness of her bedroom as he attacked her.

"You don't look so dangerous," he said, voice mocking.

Dirtbag.

Sarah raised an eyebrow. "Looks can be deceiving. I kicked your ass, so I'm obviously a bit more dangerous than you think."

Montoya's eyes narrowed, but the mocking expression never left his face. "You don't know what's coming for you, *niñita*. This is bigger than you think. You won't be able to hide from the *Alteza*."

Sarah leaned forward, her eyes never leaving his. "Your *Alteza* killed two of my friends," she hissed. "It won't happen again. I'm going to find him and make him regret that I ever learned his name."

"You don't know his true name," Montoya said with a loud, barking laugh. The sudden sound was grating in the small room. "Nobody knows his true name. *Viene por ti!*"

Sarah stood. Goosebumps raced across her skin at the man's chilling laughter. Without another word, she knocked on the door and the investigator opened it. He gave her a questioning look, but she ignored him and stalked off toward the front of the building.

Anything to escape Montoya's chilling laughter that was still ringing in her ears.

* * * * *

Arturo stood in front of the floor-to-ceiling windows in his office. They didn't afford him a grand view, thanks to the cement wall surrounding his compound.

He'd prefer a water view, with his own private beach.

Instead, he was holed up in the middle of the jungle where no one could ever find him.

Maria would have enjoyed a water view as well.

Fresh rage swept through him.

Roman Holt.

He was the reason Maria was dead. The reason Arturo had spent the last five years fleeing the U.S. government.

Arturo's revenge had only just begun.

The office door opened, and Tomas poked his head inside. "You asked to see me, *Alteza?*"

"Yes." Arturo straightened his suit jacket and returned

to his seat at the massive desk. "Is the girl dead yet?"

Tomas paled. "Uh… No, sir. Not yet."

Arturo's brows lowered. "I thought I told you to fix your mistake."

"I did, *Alteza.* That is, I tried. I sent Montoya to finish her, but he was arrested—"

Arturo rubbed his forehead. He was surrounded by incompetent fools.

"I meant, fix it *yourself.*" He stood. "Take care of Montoya and the girl, and do it with your own hands, *tonto incompetente.*"

Tomas bowed hastily. "I will, *Alteza.*"

He started to back out of the room.

"And Tomas?"

"Sir?"

Arturo pinned him with a look that promised retribution. "Don't fail me this time."

Tomas looked as if he was going to piss his pants. "Yes, *Alteza.*"

CHAPTER 10

EMMETT CAUGHT UP TO SARAH before she reached the doors of the police station. She knew he would, and she was prepared when he grabbed her arm and yanked her to a stop. He turned her around to face him. His expression was torn between fury and concern. "What was that back there?"

Sarah pulled her arm away and averted her gaze. "None of your concern."

"The hell it isn't!" When several officers looked in their direction, he turned his back to them and lowered his voice. "What have you gotten yourself mixed up in?"

Sarah stubbornly kept her eyes on her feet, refusing to answer him.

After a tense silence, Emmett grabbed her arm again and hauled her out of the police station and down the street to his waiting SUV. He deposited her in the passenger seat and then crossed around the front of the vehicle.

Sarah glowered at him, breathing deeply as she applied pressure to her side with one hand. If she was in better shape, she'd let him have it for treating her like an errant child.

But the pain radiating from her bandage meant she was probably still bleeding. She needed to check it soon.

She thought about mentioning it to Emmett but quickly dismissed the idea. He'd think it was a trick to get out of answering his questions.

And since Owen had dropped her off at the station earlier that morning, Emmett was her only ride home. She couldn't afford to piss him off.

He started the SUV and pulled away from the curb. Even though his face was a mask of fury, it didn't affect his driving. He expertly wove in and out of traffic, going exactly the speed limit, and kept his eyes on the road.

"We're going to the office," he said finally. "And you're going to tell me exactly what's going on."

Sarah didn't answer. Instead, she stared out the window and tried to think of nothing at all. She was so tired.

Tired of wondering who Altez was, tired of fighting not to be killed at every turn, tired of keeping secrets from her family.

And most of all, she was tired of the persistent ache that had settled in her chest since Ryan's murder. She just wanted the whole thing to be over.

Could she tell Emmett everything?

He was a former Navy SEAL; it's not like he was an easy person to kill. He, Owen and Chance had all endured training precisely for these types of situations.

In her head, Sarah knew that... but her heart didn't agree.

Her heart told her that if she lost another person she loved, she'd never recover.

By the time they arrived at the ESI office, the sun had barely risen, and Sarah was functioning on little more than an hour of sleep.

The office was full despite the early hour.

Sarah nodded half-heartedly at the team – minus Roman – sitting in the conference room as Emmett led her down the hall and into his office. She dropped into the leather chair across from his desk, careful to keep her expression neutral so as not to alert him of the pain in her side that was growing increasingly bothersome.

She was definitely still bleeding, but she'd check it later.

She had other matters to attend to first.

* * * * *

Roman stormed into the ESI office.

He didn't acknowledge the team as he stalked past the conference room. They must have seen his expression, because they didn't call out a greeting either.

He was pissed.

A cryptic text from Dominick at three a.m. had told him something happened to Sarah. Dominick didn't know what; he just said Owen came racing into the building, muttering to himself about drug lords and masked men and cursing his sister's name.

Roman had driven all over this godforsaken town trying to figure out what happened. None of the Ericksons would answer their phones. The house was deserted. Nobody at the hospital.

Finally, some fool at the police station had told him Sarah just left with Emmett.

Now here Roman was, three hours later, and he'd finally caught up to them.

He slammed open the door to Emmett's office without so much as a knock. He was too pissed off and - he couldn't even admit it to himself - worried to care about decorum at that point.

Emmett and Sarah both swung their heads around to look at him in surprise.

With a single sweep of his gaze, Roman saw the frustration in his boss's eyes and the determination in Sarah's. Emmett stood behind his desk while Sarah sat in the chair across from it, one hand resting protectively on her side, just above her hip.

Her blonde hair hung loose, tumbling over her shoulders and halfway down her back, and mussed the way only sleep could do. It was longer than he would've guessed; he'd never seen it like this since she always kept it pulled back.

He wished she would wear it like this more often.

Then he noticed that her left eye was swollen shut, surrounded by a nasty purple bruise.

He wanted to murder the man who'd marred her beautiful face.

All these observations happened in the space of a breath. Roman ignored Emmett and directed his attention to Sarah. "You're lucky you're alive."

Sarah looked calm as ever, but he didn't miss the small

tremor in her free hand before she fisted it in her lap. "I'd say it was skill."

"I warned you to keep your nose out of this. You should've listened."

"Don't talk to me like I'm a child. I'm perfectly capable of taking care of myself."

Emmett looked from Roman to Sarah and back again, his expression growing more irritated. "What. The hell. Is going on?"

Sarah glared at Roman, green eyes flashing. Wordlessly threatening him not to say anything to her brother.

Well, to hell with that. Roman knew why she didn't want to tell Emmett, but this had gone beyond control.

Neither of them had a choice now.

He'd spent his entire life keeping secrets from the ones he cared about most, and it had led to his brother's death. He didn't want the same thing to happen to Sarah's family.

"You need help," he said. "Or you're going to get yourself killed."

Sarah's expression softened. For the first time, he saw vulnerability there.

The office door flew open again. Roman jumped out of the way as Owen burst into the room, breathing hard. He looked around at them, studiously avoiding Sarah. "I found something on the name."

Sarah stiffened. Her eyes flashed with hurt before the neutral mask slipped back into place.

"Sorry, Sar-Bear, but this is bigger than you." Owen cleared his throat, still avoiding her eyes. "You're in way over your head. I had to tell Emmett before something really happened to you."

Sarah glared a hole in the side of Owen's head.

"Altez isn't a drug dealer, like we first thought," Owen continued, looking at Emmett. "He's an arms dealer as well. Wanted in at least ten countries. Everybody and their dog has been looking for this guy, but he's been careful since his rise to power. Not a single country has been able to find anyone who knows his real name. We don't even know what he looks like. Just that his reach is huge. He's been linked to the assassination of several Mexican officials as well as government officials of at least six other countries. He's considered one of the most dangerous men alive."

"Human trafficking as well," Roman said.

All three Erickson siblings turned to stare at him, mouths agape.

Emmett's expression said they'd have words later, but he turned his attention back to Sarah. "How did you end up involved with this guy?"

"I'm not involved with him." Sarah's hackles rose at her brother's tone. "He killed my best friend."

"Who?" Owen asked.

"Ryan. My roommate."

"Your roommate?" Emmett echoed. "You were living with a man in New York?"

"Really? That's what you're going to focus on?" Sarah rolled her eyes. "Welcome to the twenty-first century, gentlemen. Yes, we've been living together for the past six years. Just as friends."

"Why didn't you ever tell me that?" Owen asked, looking hurt.

Sarah glared at him. "Because you can't keep a secret."

"How do you know this Altez killed your friend?" Emmett interrupted.

"The burner phone." Owen looked at Sarah. "It was Ryan's, wasn't it?"

Roman frowned. "What burner phone?"

"Sarah asked me to pull some data off a burner phone she brought back from New York. I found evidence of wire transfers from someone named Altez."

No, it couldn't be true. But the sinking feeling in his gut confirmed what his brother had done. Roman couldn't acknowledge it yet; not until he had solid proof.

"Why didn't you tell us about this as soon as it happened?" Emmett demanded of Sarah.

"Apparently I'm not good enough for ESI to bother with, so I figured I'd handle it on my own."

Emmett looked like he might explode.

"That's not why," Owen said, kneeling next to Sarah's chair. "That's not what you told me the other night."

Sarah's shoulders sagged. She suddenly looked exhausted. "No, it's not. I wanted to tell you, but every time I tried, we started arguing. And then Tom happened and... I didn't want that to happen to you too."

Emmett's expression softened. He circled his desk until he stood in front of Sarah's chair. She avoided his gaze, but he reached down and placed a hand on her shoulder. A tear slipped down her cheek, and she kept her face averted.

"What do you have to do with any of this?" Emmett asked, looking away from Sarah and meeting Roman's gaze.

All eyes turned to Roman, and his stomach dropped.

How much should he say?

Hell, he couldn't avenge Ryan's death without ESI's help.

So he'd have to tell them everything.

"Ryan was my brother. It's my fault he's dead."

CHAPTER 11

ROMAN FACED THE ERICKSON SIBLINGS, hands clasped behind his back, and waited for their reactions to his bombshell.

Owen released a huff of breath. "Well, I didn't see that one coming."

Sarah was the only one who didn't look surprised. Of course she'd been suspicious of him; she was a smart girl.

"Explain," Emmett said. His voice was gruff, but it wasn't accusatory. ESI was built on a foundation of trust, and he would never place blame until he knew all the facts.

When ESI first opened its doors, Chance and Emmett spent the first six months training the team as a unit before they took any assignments. It was important to establish a bond of friendship and trust before they risked their lives in the field. That bond had continued to strengthen throughout every mission they'd survived together.

Roman would take a bullet for any one of the men on the team, and he knew they'd do the same for him.

"Before I joined ESI, I was in special forces. Our sole

target was a drug lord by the name of Altez."

"So you know this guy," Owen said.

Roman stared at a point on the wall over Emmett's right shoulder. For a moment, he allowed the memories to come rushing back. "I spent two years undercover. First as a lowly drug dealer out of the U.S., then I moved my way up the ranks. Ryan was still in high school at the time. I was taking care of him." He paused to swallow, forcing his expression to remain impassive. "I was careful never to bring my work home, so Ryan wouldn't get involved. But when I neared the top of Altez's hierarchy, I finally learned the location of his compound. My team was sent to infiltrate it."

"So what happened?" Emmett asked.

"Things went sideways. I killed Altez's wife, and he escaped. He's been out for revenge ever since. I was forced into hiding. By that time, Ryan had moved to New York to start school. I couldn't contact him, for his own safety, so I haven't seen him since."

"How do you think he got involved, then?" Owen asked.

"I'm not sure yet. He was a nosey kid with that camera of his. Maybe he met one of my contacts and was somehow dragged into this. Looking back on it now, he never asked me for help paying for college. Maybe he was selling to pay for his tuition."

"Makes sense," Sarah murmured. She twirled the end of her hair around her fingers, her expression distant and sad.

Roman felt the urge to place an arm around her shoulders.

What the hell? That would be wildly inappropriate.

Not to mention Emmett would blow his head off before he could make contact.

"He was always disappearing, sometimes for hours at a time," Sarah continued. "Usually he told me everything, but he would never tell me where he went during those times. He always seemed to have money, even though he only worked part-time at a coffee shop. I just assumed his family was wealthy."

"We weren't. We barely got by."

"This is all beginning to make sense," Emmett said. The mantle of authority settled onto his shoulders again. He was back to being ESI's team leader. "Owen, start digging into Ryan. See if you can find a link between him and Altez. He obviously knew something that was worth killing for. We need to know what that was."

Owen nodded briskly and left the office.

Emmett looked at Sarah next. "In the meantime, you need to get off the grid. Altez is after you, which means you're not safe in town."

"I know a place a few hours from here," Roman heard himself saying. "It's a cabin that belongs to my old team lead, Jeffries. I can keep her safe there."

What a terrible, horrible, potentially disastrous idea.

Emmett shot him a shrewd look, then finally nodded. "All right. Leave now. Take a sedan out of the garage. It's unmarked and shouldn't be easily traced. I shouldn't have to tell you, but keep an eye out for tails."

"I'll call Jeffries and let him know we'll be using it."

Sarah looked between the two of them with a

flabbergasted expression. "Now wait a second," she began hotly. "Do I get a say in this?"

"No," Emmett and Roman said in unison.

Sarah scowled. "I don't even get to pack any clothes? How long am I going to be gone?"

"As long as necessary. Roman can get you whatever you need. Your life is priority one right now." Emmett's tone brooked no argument.

But of course Sarah was going to argue anyway. Roman admired her fire, even though it wasn't the time or place for it.

"This isn't fair. Ryan was my friend. I'm the one who realized something was fishy about his death. I want to help you catch this guy."

Emmett leaned forward, across his desk, and looked her in the eye. "You won't be able to help anyone if you're dead. For once in your life, do as I say."

Sarah looked like she might argue further.

Roman cleared his throat. "Sarah."

She looked up at him. Her expression was still angry, but her hands trembled in her lap.

"I know you can take care of yourself, but Altez is bigger than you can imagine. Let me help keep you safe, and we'll get to the bottom of this. But we need to go now."

After a tense moment, Sarah wilted. "Fine, I'll go. But I don't like it."

"Noted." Roman took her hand and towed her out of the room. He didn't miss Emmett's expression as his eyes locked on their clasped fingers before the door closed behind them.

With the way things were going, if Altez didn't kill him, Emmett might just finish the job.

CHAPTER 12

ROAD-TRIPPING WITH ROMAN was the last thing Sarah wanted to do, but she was too exhausted to fight about it any further. Despite her bravado, she really would like to keep her head attached to her shoulders.

Altez was turning out to be a scary dude, and if Roman was her best chance at survival, she'd have to deal with him for now.

The drive to the safe house was going to take a few hours. Apparently it was somewhere in the forest in Oregon. She settled into the passenger seat and rested her forehead against the window, staring absently at the passing scenery.

Roman was quiet, his gaze straight ahead as he drove. He appeared calm, but he had a death grip on the steering wheel and he kept glancing in the rearview mirror to make sure they weren't being followed.

He was usually cool as a cucumber, so the tension was enough to freak Sarah out.

An hour into the drive, loud vibrating sounded from Roman's pocket. He pulled out an old brick phone that looked like it was from the early 2000s.

Remarkably similar to Ryan's.

"It's nearly indestructible," he said defensively in response to her pointed look. "Holt here."

Sarah watched his face as he listened. The lines around his mouth deepened slightly, but he was too good at hiding his thoughts. Another reason he pissed Sarah off.

"I understand. Thanks." He hit a button and slid the phone back into his pocket, returning his eyes to the road.

"Well?"

"Well, what?"

"Who was that?"

"Owen."

"And?"

Roman sighed and glanced her way. "Montoya is dead. Found hanging in his cell this morning."

Sarah shivered. "I guess that investigator was lying when he said the police could protect him."

"Guess so. They're trying to find evidence of foul play, but they won't."

"Altez is too good."

Roman dipped his head in grim acknowledgment.

Sarah let the silence stretch for a moment. "How do you think Ryan got involved in all this? He isn't... wasn't... a bad person."

Roman didn't answer at first. She thought he would ignore her question, but finally he spoke. "Our parents died when Ryan was eight years old. We were placed in foster care. Luckily we were never separated, but some of those homes weren't exactly desirable. That's where this scar came from." He touched the scar that slashed through his left eye.

Sarah's heart ached for the young Roman and Ryan. She couldn't imagine what their childhood must have been like.

The mystery surrounding Roman's personality dissipated a little.

"I tried to protect him as best I could, but I was only thirteen. When I was old enough, I joined the military so we could get out of foster care. It took a lot of time and paperwork, but I managed to get custody of Ryan. I gave him a place to live while he was in high school and I was away. When I began my undercover work with the special forces, I couldn't keep Ryan completely in the dark. He was too curious, always getting himself into situations he couldn't get out of."

"That sounds like him."

A ghost of a smile passed over Roman's features. "You remind me of him in some ways."

"I don't... *always* get into trouble I can't get out of."

"Right. You're more capable than Emmett gives you credit for." He glanced at her and smiled. "If I'd been smarter, I would've sent Ryan away so he couldn't get anywhere near the shit I was into. But I was arrogant. I thought I could protect him from anything. And now he's dead."

Roman's right hand gripped the gearshift so tightly that Sarah thought he would break it. She placed her hand over his and squeezed lightly. "It wasn't your fault, Roman. You're a smart guy. You must know that."

Roman didn't respond. A muscle worked in his jaw.

She bit her lip. This was foreign territory. She didn't *do* emotional moments like this; they just weren't her thing. "Hey. Speaking of situations he couldn't get himself out of, do you know about Ryan's obsession with his camera?"

"Yeah," he murmured. "It started with a photography class in high school. I got him that DSLR for his eighteenth birthday."

"He took that thing everywhere. One time, he took pictures of this old librarian at NYU's library. She was a hag, always yelling at us to be quiet while we studied. He took a picture of her while she was picking her nose behind her desk. She thought nobody was looking. She chased him halfway across campus before she finally flagged down campus police. They made him delete the photo and write an apology letter to the librarian. I laughed at him for weeks afterward because she would give him the dirtiest look every time we walked past."

The corner of Roman's mouth twitched and he broke into a smile. "That sounds like him."

Sarah gaped at him. When he smiled like that, he looked... sexy.

She cleared her throat. "Uh, yeah, he did stuff like that all the time."

Roman's smile remained in place when he glanced over at her. "Thanks."

Sarah's heart skipped around in her chest. She smiled back at him. "You're welcome."

* * * * *

Six and a half hours later, Roman finally pulled the sedan off the highway in Mt. Hood National Forest.

They'd made a quick stop in Seattle to pick up a few essentials; a change of clothes for Sarah, some toothbrushes, and a few food items to get them through the next few days.

Sarah had fallen asleep not even an hour into the drive. Roman had spent the majority of the trip alternating between watching her and watching the road behind them. Even in sleep, she looked exhausted. A dark circle marred the skin underneath her uninjured eye, and she was more pale than usual.

Roman wondered what she was dreaming about. Judging from the crease in her forehead, it wasn't anything good. No surprise, considering the events of the past few weeks.

He stopped the car in front of a small metal gate on a rarely-used side road. It was secured with a single padlock, which he unlocked with a small key he kept in his wallet.

When he returned to the driver's seat after locking the gate behind them, Sarah was sitting up. She looked at him blearily, stifling a yawn behind her hand. "Are we here?"

"Almost."

The car crawled through the winding, narrow dirt road for another two miles before the safe house came into view. It was a tiny cabin that was almost invisible in the thick undergrowth and dense trees.

Roman's gut churned. Last time he'd been here, he'd been running for his life. Now he was running for Sarah's.

That cabin was too damn small for two people.

He grabbed the bags from the backseat and opened Sarah's door for her. Her face distorted into a grimace as she climbed out. As she straightened, the color fled from her cheeks and she swayed.

"Whoa." Roman grabbed her arm to steady her. "What's wrong?"

Sarah looked guiltily up at him. "I may have neglected to do something…"

"What?"

She lifted the hem of her t-shirt. The bandage covering her wound was soaked red. Blood dripped down the pale skin of her side, disappearing under the waistband of her jeans.

"Damn it, Sarah." Roman dropped the bags and put an arm around her shoulders. "Why didn't you say something?"

"So many things were happening at once. I kind of forgot."

"Kind of-?" Roman unlocked the front door of the cabin and threw it open. He ushered her to sit on the tiny couch in front of the fireplace. "Don't move. I'll be right back."

He jogged outside and grabbed the bags, locked the car, and returned to the cabin.

Once he'd locked the front door behind him, he dropped the bags on the counter in the kitchen and rummaged through the cupboards, muttering under his breath.

"I'll be fine," she called from the living room. "I just need fluids and some rest. It's just a little blood loss."

"Just a little blood loss," he mimicked in a high voice,

still under his breath. "And you wanted to be a doctor. Holy hell."

He returned to the living room, first aid kit in hand, to see her leaning back against the couch, eyes half-closed.

"Hey. No sleeping until I know what we're dealing with."

She sighed and opened her eyes. "Really, I'm fine."

"Really, you're not. Lift up your shirt."

She raised an eyebrow. "Are you coming on to me?"

"Oh, you're a comedian too?" Roman lifted her shirt and she held it while he unwrapped the bandage around her waist. The wound was still oozing blood, so the gauze came easily away from her skin.

It would've been better if it had crusted over.

Roman set the bloody rags on the coffee table and peered at her wound. "You pulled your stitches."

"Yeah, I figured. All thanks to Altez's hitman."

"You need stitches. The bleeding isn't stopping."

"Fine. Hand me a needle." She held out an expectant hand.

"I don't think so." Roman swatted her hand away. "I'll do it. I was the medical technician on this team before you came along, you know."

"I'm perfectly capable-"

"Yeah, yeah, you can take care of yourself. Give it a rest."

She shot him an irritated look. "Just do it already."

Roman ducked his head, hiding a smile, and got to work. She didn't make a sound as he placed three neat stitches to seal her wound. Once he was finished, he took one look at her gray complexion and handed her a couple pills. "Take these. You've lost too much blood."

She peered at them. "What are they? Iron pills?"

"Yep. They'll prevent you from going into hypovolemic shock. Now sit here and rest. I'll make us something to eat."

An hour later, they sat cross-legged at the coffee table with steaming plates of food in front of them.

Sarah inhaled deeply. "This smells heavenly. What kind of chicken is this?"

"Secret recipe." Roman handed her a fork.

"Really? Do tell. I love a good secret."

"Okay, I'll tell you, but you must vow to take it to your grave." Roman waited until she nodded her agreement. "The secret is the five-year-old lemon pepper I found in the cupboard. You sprinkle a bit of that on there, fry it up, and there you go. Spices age like wine, you know. Those expiration dates are just a government cover-up."

Sarah blinked at him, shocked.

It had been a long time since he'd joked with anyone, but what had possessed him to decide that now was a good time? Sarah could have been killed, either by Montoya or by the blood loss, and they were on the run from an all-powerful Mexican cartel lord who wanted to kill them both.

Was he losing his mind?

Sarah burst into a fit of laughter.

It was Roman's turn to stare in shock. The sound thawed something in his chest that had been frozen for a long time. He couldn't hide the grin that split his face.

"You know, Roman," she said, wiping tears from her eyes. "With a sense of humor, you're almost the whole package."

"Almost? What am I missing?"

"If I told you, where's the fun in that?" She leaned back against the base of the couch, her eyes traveling over the small interior of the cabin. "So how did you know about this place?"

Roman followed her gaze. "It's from my undercover days. When my cover was blown, Jeffries, my team lead, sent me here. It's been in his family for generations. Only used for emergencies."

"Does he know we're here?"

"Yeah. I couldn't take the chance that he might happen to be in the area, and shoot us as intruders." Roman sighed. "I spent a lot of time here when I first went underground."

Sarah put down her fork. The glow of the fireplace bathed the right side of her face in soft light.

Despite the dark bruise covering her eye, she looked beautiful.

"What was it like to be undercover?"

Roman cleared his throat, forcing himself to look away from her and down to his plate. "Hard. Not like the movies would lead you to believe."

"How do you mean?"

"I did a lot of horrible things; things that went against what I believe in." He shrugged. He didn't want to stray into the dark recesses of his past. It took a long time to put all that behind him. "The mission, the greater good, always came first."

Sarah shivered. "I can't even imagine being in that position. How did you survive when Altez found out about you?"

"I killed his man before he could kill me." Roman waited to see her reaction. Many women would think he's a monster, but Sarah just looked impressed.

"What happened after that?"

"I wandered. I couldn't go back to the forces. Jeffries made sure I was honorably discharged, but I still had a target on my back. Ryan had his own life and I didn't want to put him in danger. I lost my purpose for a while. But then Emmett found and recruited me."

They'd met at a bar in Seattle. At the time, Roman thought it was merely by chance, but he knew now that Emmett searched out each one of them with the goal of recruiting them to ESI's team. To this day, Roman still didn't know how Emmett had found him.

"ESI gave me a purpose," he said. "I don't think I'd be here today without them."

"I'm glad you're here," Sarah said softly. The flames from the fireplace danced in her green eyes. "I'm glad Altez didn't kill you."

She was sitting so close to him, their hips almost touching. A golden halo surrounded her blonde hair, which framed her perfect face.

Well, almost perfect.

Roman hesitated, then gently touched the purple bruise around her right eye. His fingers moved of their own accord, down her cheek and around to the back of her neck, tangling in her hair.

"He almost killed you, too," he said, voice as soft as hers.

"I know. I keep replaying it in my head, over and over."

Roman's hand tightened in her hair. He didn't want her to be afraid.

If he hadn't tried to take on Altez, Sarah wouldn't be living with the dark shadows he saw in her eyes. Ryan wouldn't be dead. Roman would've had a normal life and a normal relationship with his brother.

But not a relationship with this woman. They never would have met.

It was probably the stress of the last couple weeks, but Sarah was leaning toward him. He was drawn to her like a magnet. He couldn't stop himself even if he wanted to.

And he didn't. He didn't want to stop at all.

"Let me help you forget," he murmured, and lowered his mouth to hers.

CHAPTER 13

SARAH COULDN'T THINK. She didn't know how to react.

Roman's lips were on hers and they were warm and soft and gentle. Their bodies were so close that she could feel the heat coming off him. Her hands settled on his chest. His heart thumped steadily through the fabric of his shirt.

This was a horrible idea.

In the morning, she'd realize what a mistake this was.

But right now, all she wanted was to feel his hands on her skin. To feel more than the cold emptiness that had been yawning inside of her for weeks now.

Roman's arms went around her, one on the small of her back, one tangled in her hair. He tugged until her hair came loose of its binding and tumbled down past her shoulders.

"I've wanted to do that since the first time I saw you," he murmured against her lips. "You shouldn't keep this beautiful hair pulled back."

Sarah's eyes fluttered open, and she got lost in his gaze.

How could she ever think Roman was cold?

In the past 24 hours, he'd proved he was the opposite.

"Before you knew I was Ryan's best friend?"

"From the very first time I saw you at the ESI office. The night you came in with Bellamy." Roman fingered her hair absently, tucking a wayward strand behind her ear. "I loved how you went toe-to-toe with Emmett. You were fearless."

"Emmett's not as scary as he thinks he is."

"The team is scared spitless of him."

Sarah chuckled. Any one of the men on the team could kill someone with their bare hands, but they cowered like little girls in the face of their team leader.

"Let me tell you a secret." She leaned closer, her lips just a hair away from his ear. "Emmett cares more than anyone you'll ever meet. He seems scary, but he's as soft as they come. He just has a hard time showing it."

"Mm. Enough about your brother." His lips descended on hers again. "I want to focus on you right now."

Sarah's toes curled as a delicious shiver spread through her.

"I've wanted this too," she admitted a moment later.

"Mm?"

"Since I first saw you."

"Mm."

Ryan's face flashed in her mind. Sarah froze, her hands on Roman's chest. She wanted to give in to the moment, to melt into Roman's arms and forget everything else.

But before she did, he deserved to know the truth.

"Roman..."

His head lifted at the sudden shakiness in her voice. "What is it, sweetheart?"

"I... was on the scene when Ryan..." Mortifying tears filled her eyes and she ducked her head before he could see. "I saw him before he died."

Roman went still, but he didn't interrupt her. She didn't dare look at his face. Surely he would hate her for not mentioning it sooner.

"I tried to save him, but I was too late. I looked into his eyes, Roman, and I couldn't save him. I watched him die, watched the light fade from his eyes while I did CPR. I was too late. I'm always too late." She couldn't breathe around the lump in her throat. "Ryan and Tom; I see their faces every time I close my eyes. I'm so scared it will happen to someone else that I care about. Emmett, Chance, Bellamy, Owen... You."

She waited, drowning in the silence, for him to respond.

After a moment, he put his fingers under her chin and lifted her head until she was forced to meet his eyes. She saw no condemnation there; only compassion.

"Sarah," he said softly. "You're a lot stronger than everyone gives you credit for."

And he kissed her.

It was soft, sweet, sincere. Her hands fisted in his shirt.

"I just want to forget it all. I don't want to see their faces anymore."

Roman's eyes drifted over her face. With one finger, he caressed her cheek, her bruised and swollen eye. "Sweetheart, you've seen more violence and death than anyone should have to. I would take it away in a heartbeat if

I could."

His lips barely brushed her bruised skin.

Sarah shivered. His touch was so gentle, as if she'd break if he wasn't careful.

"In time, you'll get used to seeing their faces. They're a part of you now, so they'll never completely go away. However indirectly, I'm responsible for that. I got you into this by tangling with Altez all those years ago. I'll make sure you make it out. I promise."

The words weren't as comforting as he probably wanted them to be. Instead, it sounded like the final promise of a man condemned to death.

No, it was her imagination. Roman wouldn't allow himself to fall to a man like Altez.

She pulled on his shirt, pulled his head down so she could meld her lips to his. "Let's not talk about sad stuff anymore," she said softly.

Without another word, he put one arm around her back and the other underneath her knees, and he scooped her up and into his arms.

Any other time, Sarah would have protested the archaic princess-hold, but she was too vulnerable and heartsick to care at the moment. Instead, she rested her head against his shoulder as he carried her into the bedroom.

* * * * *

Roman woke to a sound that shouldn't be there.

He'd spent a long time in this cabin; he knew the night

sounds better than his own heartbeat.

This sound wasn't part of the forest.

It was boots crunching in the dirt.

Roman shook Sarah's shoulder gently. She mumbled something and turned her back to him, settling into the pillow.

Shit.

Roman rolled off the mattress and retrieved his SIG from the nightstand. The cabin key was next to it, and he tucked it into his waistband.

The chilly September air gave him goosebumps as he left the tiny bedroom and entered the main area of the cabin.

He was only in his boxers, but there was no time to put pants on.

Sarah would be safe in the bedroom. There were no windows. The only entrance to the cabin was the front door, and they'd have to go through Roman to get there.

Roman slipped his feet into his boots and gently eased open the front door. Luckily, the area was illuminated by the full moon above.

No need for his night goggles.

Roman stepped outside and closed the door behind him, locking it for good measure. Then he crept around the side of the cabin and blended into the trees.

He stopped to listen.

The slight static of a radio gave away the enemy's position.

Roman crept up behind a man crouched in the bushes and choked him out before he could even react.

He yanked the earpiece out of his ear and shoved it into his own.

"Making my way around the south side," a fuzzy voice said. "Jones, any movement?"

A moment of silence.

"Jones?"

Roman looked down at the man at his feet. This must be Jones.

No other voices on the radio.

There were only two intruders.

Altez was slipping.

Roman ran around to the south side of the cabin, his gun at the ready. The second intruder was crouching behind a wide tree, fumbling with the radio at his hip.

He froze when Roman's gun pressed to the back of his head.

"Not the greeting I was hoping for this morning," Roman said conversationally. "Put your hands up and turn around slowly."

The man obeyed.

In the light from the moon, Roman could see that the man wasn't Hispanic.

He was clearly American.

Not only that, but he was well-equipped in tactical gear, including night-vision goggles.

Was Altez recruiting ex-military mercenaries now? That was new.

"Who sent you?"

The man scowled and spit at Roman's feet.

"Well, that's not very nice." Roman thumbed the safety

on his SIG. "If you're not willing to talk, I guess I'll put you down here."

Sweat broke out on the man's forehead, but he didn't speak.

Roman pressed his finger to the trigger.

One second passed, then two, then three...

"All right, you called my bluff." Roman pulled the gun away from the man's chest. "I'm not in the mood to kill anyone today."

Instead, he walked the man back over to his unconscious comrade. Once he was sure all weapons were stripped from both of them, he gagged them and tied them to a tree with a length of rope he found in one of their bags.

Then he returned to the cabin. Once he made it back inside, he grabbed his phone and dialed Emmett's number.

The cabin was compromised.

He couldn't think about how that happened. Right now, he needed to worry about getting Sarah to a safe place.

Emmett answered. "I was just about to call you."

"The safe house is compromised."

"What?" Urgency painted Emmett's voice. "Is Sarah okay?"

"We're fine. I neutralized the threat. But we need to move. I'm going to find a new location for us, but – "

"Don't worry about it."

"What?"

Emmett let out a deep breath. "We have a situation."

"What's going on?"

"My mom's gone."

Roman's skin turned cold. He cast a quick glance at the

cracked bedroom door. "What are you talking about?"

"She's missing. She went out to grab some groceries and we haven't heard from her since."

"Didn't someone go with her?"

"Owen was supposed to, but she left before he could get home." A harsh breath sounded in the line, and Emmett muttered a low curse.

Roman swallowed hard. It was more emotion than he'd ever heard from his boss. He made sure his voice was steady before he spoke again. "Okay. What's our next move?"

"I don't know."

Sarah was right; Emmett cared more than he led everyone else to believe. He was usually the leader in every situation, clear-headed and assured in every step he took. For the first time in ESI's history, he seemed at a loss.

Roman cleared his throat. He had to take charge. Emmett was too emotionally involved in this to have a clear head.

But then again, wasn't Roman emotionally involved now too?

It didn't matter.

"I know Altez. He never does anything without thinking of the benefit to himself. He took your mom to flush Sarah out. When he's ready, he'll contact her for an exchange."

"But what does he want from Sarah? She doesn't even know who he is."

"It doesn't matter. Altez is a prideful man. She is a loose end that needs to be exterminated. Now that the situation has changed, we need to meet and regroup."

"We need a plan."

"Yeah." Roman glanced at the bedroom door again. He did not want to wake Sarah up with more bad news. "If you've got any police contacts near here, send them to pick up these two bozos that tried to get the jump on me. I'll grab Sarah and we'll head your way."

"I'll take care of it. See you soon. Be safe."

Roman hung up and dropped his phone onto the couch. This was not how he'd imagined this morning going.

His version had included pancakes in bed.

Instead, he had to wake Sarah up and tell her that one of her worst fears had come to pass.

Sarah's breathing was still deep and even when Roman entered the bedroom. He sat on the edge of the bed and leaned over to brush her hair away from her face.

"Sweetheart," he said softly.

Sarah stirred and smiled sweetly, eyes still closed, and turned her face into his hand as if she needed his touch.

His heart did a somersault in his chest.

Slowly, her eyes fluttered open and she blinked at him. "Hi. What time is it?"

"Late. Or early, depending on how you look at it."

She smiled and closed her eyes again.

"Sweetheart, you need to wake up. I just heard from Emmett."

Just like that, she was wide awake. She sat up and the covers fell away from her shoulders.

Roman's eyes were immediately drawn downward. Damn, why had he woken her up again? His mind went completely blank.

Belatedly, Sarah remembered her nakedness and yanked the blanket back up over her chest. Her cheeks were bright red.

It was adorable.

"What did Emmett say?"

Roman's suddenly sober expression must have given something away. Sarah immediately leaped out of bed and began pulling on her clothing. She moved remarkably well considering her wound. When she was dressed, she turned to him expectantly.

No time to sugarcoat it. "Your mother is missing."

All color drained from Sarah's face and she staggered as if she'd been hit. She placed a hand on the wall to steady herself. "How?"

"Not sure yet." Roman pulled on a pair of pants, threw what little belongings they had into a bag and hiked it over his shoulder. "We need to regroup, so we're going back to La Conner."

Sarah nodded, pulling her tousled hair into a ponytail. "Let's go."

CHAPTER 14

SOMEHOW, THEIR TRIP BACK to La Conner took four hours instead of six and a half. They must have broken a hundred traffic laws to achieve that feat, but Sarah was grateful for Roman's adept driving.

If it meant getting back home even one minute sooner, it was worth it.

Everyone was already gathered in the lounge when they arrived at ESI headquarters. Emmett and Chance paced in front of the projector screen, their brows knit in identical worried frowns. Bellamy perched in an armchair nearby, her hands clasped tightly in her lap. Dominick and Cameron sat on the leather couch in the center of the room, weapons in their laps and grim expressions on their faces.

They all looked up when Sarah burst into the lobby. Bellamy stood up, her face a mask of concern and sympathy, and Sarah rushed over to give her a hug. They clung to each other for a moment, needing the comfort only another female could provide.

"Status?" Roman asked from behind Sarah.

"Nothing yet," Emmett said.

Sarah pulled away from Bellamy to look at her brothers. Emmett looked stoic as usual, but there were dark circles under his eyes. Chance didn't look any better.

Wordlessly, Sarah went to Emmett and he opened his arms. She walked into his embrace and held him tightly.

Petty arguments had no place in this situation.

"I'm sorry," Sarah said, pulling back to look up at him. His face swam in her vision. "If I hadn't gone looking into things, Mom would still be here. Safe."

Roman's hand rested on her shoulder and gave a reassuring squeeze. "We'll find her."

Sarah shot him a grateful look over her shoulder. Warmth spread through her from his touch, providing the comfort she badly needed.

Emmett nodded above her. "Yes. We'll find her."

"I found something!"

Everyone turned to the hallway at Owen's triumphant voice. He strode into the lounge area, his blond hair sticking up in all directions. He had dark circles under his eyes - clearly, he hadn't slept - but he was grinning from ear to ear.

"What is it?" Emmett asked.

Owen plugged a flash drive into a nearby tablet and turned on the projector. An Excel spreadsheet appeared on the screen.

Sarah stared at it, as did everyone else. "What are we looking at?"

"I've been digging, trying to find a link between Ryan and Altez." Owen gestured at the numbers. "He's been receiving deposits into his bank account, and not small ones either. I managed to trace them to a Swiss bank account, and traced that to one of Altez's known aliases."

"So maybe Ryan was dealing for Altez," Chance said.

"Maybe. But these numbers are really large for a minor drug dealer. I don't have the answer to that yet, but I do have something else."

Everyone looked at him expectantly.

"I have some contacts with the CIA from when they tried to recruit me. I reached out to them." Owen ignored the raised eyebrows sent his way. "They found a name."

"A name? Like Altez's real name?" Roman asked, incredulous. "My higher-ups always told me we didn't know his real name."

"I don't know if it's his real name, but it must be important. My contact at the CIA said it was buried under so many firewalls it was kind of ridiculous." Owen paused, allowing the silence to stretch. "Arturo Montez."

Sarah glanced around the room. The name didn't seem to mean anything to anyone, including Roman.

"What were you able to find out about him?" Emmett asked, unimpressed.

"Not much. He's from Spain, had a rough childhood, and was pretty much a criminal by the time he could walk." Owen shrugged, and for the first time, he looked disappointed that he didn't have more news. "He's covered his tracks well."

"Okay. We have a name." Emmett's jaw was set as he looked around the room. "Owen, keep digging. See what you can find out. Everyone needs to be ready to move. Whoever this guy is, he's extremely dangerous."

"In the meantime-" Chance began.

'Eye of the Tiger' filled the room. Everyone fell silent.

It was a cell phone.

It took Sarah a moment to realize it was hers. She fumbled with her purse, fingers suddenly shaking, and pulled it out. It was a blocked number. Her breath caught in her throat.

Roman stepped forward and put his hand over hers. "It's okay." His voice was steady, reassuring. "Answer it. We have to find out what he wants."

Half praying it was a telemarketer, Sarah pushed the button and held the phone to her ear. Everyone in the room watched her expectantly. "Hello?"

"Sarah Erickson." The voice on the line was raspy, but the Latin accent was unmistakable.

"Yes. Who is this?" But Sarah already knew. It was the man who would haunt her nightmares for the rest of her life.

"If you want your mother alive, you will bring the phone and the SD card to these coordinates in two hours."

Owen gestured at her to keep Altez talking. He jerked a pair of headphones onto his ears and stared at the tablet in his hand.

"W-What coordinates? What SD card? I don't know-"

"Come alone, and don't be late. Or your mother dies."

Click.

"Dammit." Owen dropped the tablet onto the couch in disgust. "I couldn't get a ping on his location."

Sarah sank down onto the couch, clutching her phone to her chest. Her heart was about two seconds away from bursting out of her.

So that was Altez. The sound of her name in his smooth accent made her want to crawl in a hole and hide until her brothers took care of him.

But that wasn't her style.

Roman dropped onto the cushion next to her and pulled her hand into his lap. His thumb rubbed soothing circles on her skin.

Emmett cleared his throat. His eyes flashed to Sarah's lap. "What SD card are they talking about?"

"I don't know. I don't have-" Sarah stopped and gasped.

"What is it?" Roman asked.

"I think I know what he wants. Owen, did you bring my bag?"

"Yeah, call me pack mule. It's in the car." He tossed her the keys.

Sarah grabbed her duffle bag out of the back seat and lugged it inside the office. She dropped it on the coffee table in the middle of the room. Everyone stared at her as she unzipped it and dumped the contents onto the coffee table.

"What are you looking for?" Dominick asked.

"This." Sarah picked up Ryan's camera and held it up for everyone to see.

"A camera?" Chance asked. "Why would Altez want that?"

"Not just any camera."

"Ryan's most prized possession," Roman finished for her. His dark eyes were stark when they met hers.

Sarah wanted to hug him, but there was no time for that. She opened the small compartment on the side of the camera and pulled out the SD card. "Some guy showed up at my apartment while I was packing. He claimed to work with Ryan. He was looking for an SD card. I made some excuses and got the guy to leave. I checked the card, but it says the file is corrupted. I didn't think anything of it, but maybe..." She held it out to Owen. "Can you see what's on it?"

Owen nodded and disappeared down the hallway to his lab.

"What are we going to do about the exchange?" Chance asked.

Roman walked to the front of the room to stand by Chance and Emmett. "We need to send a team to the extraction point to intercept them."

"No," Sarah said sharply. She swallowed hard when everyone turned to look at her. "He said to come alone."

"We can't send you in there alone," Emmett said gently.

"This is Mom. We can't gamble with her life like that. We need to follow his instructions exactly, or he'll kill her."

Owen poked his head back into the main room. "The files are encrypted," he reported. "I looked at the coordinates they sent. It's an abandoned airstrip in the forest. Used in World War 2, but not since. Very remote. It'll take about an hour to get there."

Chance and Emmett shared a look. "We don't have time to argue about this," Chance said finally. "If we're going to make it to the exchange on time, we need to get moving. Sarah, can you handle this?"

"She can handle this," Roman said.

Sarah stared at him, shocked.

He gave her a firm nod. "You've proven that you can take care of yourself in the field. And we'll have your back. I'll make sure nothing happens to you."

Gratitude settled in Sarah's chest and expanded, warming her from the inside out. Damn, it felt good to have someone believe in her.

She smiled at Roman and nodded. "I can do this."

Emmett looked like he was about to have a heart attack.

Sarah turned to him next. "You're going to have to trust me. This isn't me wanting to play the hero. Please understand that, Emmett. I got Mom, all of you, into this." Her gaze locked with Roman's. "I need to make sure she gets out of it."

Roman gave her a short nod.

"All right," Emmett said. "But you'll go wired. We'll be nearby, ready to converge if necessary."

"Deal."

Owen came back into the lobby. "I can't crack these files. I don't have enough time. I copied them over to my computer though, so I'll keep working on them while you're gone."

Emmett nodded, then clapped his hands together and addressed the team. "All right, get prepped. Cameron, stock the SUV. Dominick, you're on weapons. Roman, I want to see you and Chance in my office. We need to study the area and determine points of entry."

Everyone scattered, leaving Sarah and Bellamy alone.

Bellamy crossed the room and dropped onto the couch next to Sarah. "Your mom's going to be okay."

Sarah swallowed hard. "Yeah."

"Can I give you some advice?" Bellamy reached up and unhooked the silver chain around her neck. She held it up, showing Sarah a rotating dove pendant, and then clasped it around Sarah's neck. "Altez is a lot like the criminals I dealt with back in Portland. Don't trust him to keep his word. Be ready for anything."

Sarah touched the silver pendant. It held a tracker that Owen had used to find Bellamy when she was kidnapped. It was comforting and terrifying at the same time.

She really hoped she wouldn't have to use it.

"Thanks," she said, and gave Bellamy a hug.

"Promise me you'll make it back for my wedding," Bellamy said fiercely when they pulled apart.

Sarah couldn't think of anything to say to that, so she just hugged her friend again. She didn't want to make a promise she might not be able to keep.

CHAPTER 15

OWEN WASN'T KIDDING.

The airstrip was literally in the middle of a forest with nothing around for miles. Emmett stopped the SUV caravan about five miles away and everyone got out.

Sarah stood beside the front vehicle and wiped her sweaty palms on her pants. The team had dressed her for the occasion, in black pants, a black t-shirt, and black combat boots. She wore a bulky bulletproof vest and her hair was in a tight bun so it couldn't be grabbed by an attacker. Her Glock was in its holster at her ankle, and she had a knife tucked into a pocket in her pants. The wire and its battery pack were cold against her skin, taped underneath her shirt.

The team huddled in a circle to go over the plan again, even though they'd gone over it a hundred times via radio on the way up.

Then it was time.

Dominick and Cameron gave her nods of respect and quiet wishes of good luck, then hopped into the third SUV, the last one in the caravan.

Chance hugged her first, followed by Emmett. When Emmett pulled back, his green eyes blazed at her. "You be careful," he growled. "At the first sign of trouble, you run and let us take care of the rest. Do you understand me?"

Sarah's stomach clenched. "I will."

Her brothers left her and climbed into the second SUV, leaving her alone with Roman.

To the passing observer, Roman's expression was impassive as he stared down at her, but she was starting to know him better. She could read the tension lines around his mouth and the muscles clenched in his jaw.

"If I could haul you over my shoulder and get you far away from his, I would," he said quietly.

Sarah smiled at him. "I thought you said I could take care of myself."

"You can. But that doesn't mean I won't worry."

Sarah took a deep breath and shook out her arms. "I'll see you in a few."

"Be careful. Please be careful."

They stood awkwardly for a moment.

This could be the last time Sarah saw him. Why was she so worried about appearances?

Ah, screw it.

She threw herself into his arms. If he was surprised, he didn't show it. He held her tight, and when she pulled back, he crushed his lips against hers. She didn't open her eyes until they broke apart.

She felt like a prisoner on death row. Did he feel the same way?

"Roman," she said. "Thank you."

"For what?"

"For following me. For protecting me. For last night."

Roman's arms tightened around her. "Thank me when you get back. Be careful. Take care of yourself."

"I will."

Sarah smiled at him one last time, then climbed into the lead SUV, her heart thundering in her chest. She started the engine and roared away before Roman could see the tears streaming down her face.

* * * * *

The road leading to the airstrip was cracked and riddled with potholes. Sarah took it slow, carefully maneuvering around the obstacles. It would be just her luck to get a flat tire when she had only five minutes to make it to the exchange.

The trees thinned and she entered a large clearing. The airstrip stretched in front of her, with a small jet parked on the pavement. Two men stood in front of the stairs, a woman between them.

Mom.

"I see her," Sarah muttered, careful not to move her lips. The guys didn't have a visual, so they were relying on her to describe what she saw. "She's standing next to a plane. Two hostiles, as far as I can tell."

Sarah parked the SUV about fifty yards from the two men and climbed out. She recognized one of them; he was the one she'd shot in the leg. She smiled grimly at the white bandage wrapped around his thigh. He leaned heavily on his other leg, his expression hostile as he watched her approach.

Sarah locked eyes with her mother. She looked uninjured, but her hands were secured in front of her with plastic zip ties.

Time to get to work.

"Show them the phone and the SD card," Roman instructed. His voice crackled in her earpiece. He was all business now, thank goodness.

Any other time, she'd be excited to be working in the field.

But not with her mother's life on the line.

Sarah pulled out the cell phone and the SD card, holding them in the air for the two men to see. "Release my mother. I'll leave these here and you can retrieve them."

"Too far," the uninjured man said. "Walk forward."

Sarah took a few steps closer, her heart pounding in her ears.

"Keep your distance," Roman warned.

"Closer," the man demanded.

"That's far enough." Sarah was impressed with how steady her voice was. "Let her go."

The injured man shook Mary's arm roughly. She let out a small cry of pain. The man pulled a gun and pressed it to her temple. "Come here or I'll blow her brains out."

"Okay, stop! Don't hurt her."

"Sarah, don't," Roman snapped in her earpiece.

As if she had a choice.

Sarah swallowed hard and quickly closed the distance

between them, until she was only a few feet away. She held out the phone and the SD card. "Take them and let her go."

The uninjured man yanked the items out of her hands.

"I did as you asked. Now let her go."

The injured man smiled and, with his thumb, turned off the safety to the handgun held to Mary's temple. "Get on the plane."

Sarah froze. In her earpiece, Roman shouted orders, but she couldn't understand him through the static and the roaring in her own ears.

Mary shook her head at Sarah, her eyes pleading.

Her father. Ryan. Tom.

They were dead, in the ground, with nobody who could save them.

This was what Sarah had wanted. A chance to make a difference, to save someone before they got hurt.

Calm settled over her. She smiled at Mary. "I love you."

"Sarah, stop!" Roman's voice was no longer calm. It was frantic, pleading. "Don't you dare get on that plane!"

The injured man shook Mary again, nearly pulling her arm out of her socket. Mary whimpered. Tears dripped down her cheeks.

Sarah stepped forward, hands in the air. "Okay, I'm getting on the plane. You've got me. Let her go."

The uninjured man grabbed Sarah's arm and started dragging her toward the steps that led into the jet. Before he could usher her up, Sarah planted her feet and turned back. "Let her go."

The injured man scowled and released Mary's arm. "Run."

Mary hesitated for a fraction of a second. Her eyes found Sarah's, and she looked like she was going to do something stupid.

A heartbeat passed.

Sarah mouthed, "Go. Please."

Mary let out a sob, then she finally obeyed. She stumbled away from the injured man and ran toward the SUV.

The man lifted his gun and pointed it at her back.

"No!" Sarah yanked her arm away and dove toward the injured man. Her knife slid easily from her pants and she slashed at his back. He turned, snarling, and swung the gun in her direction, but she tackled him before he could fire.

They both went down. He landed on top and tried to pin her arms to her sides with his knees. Sarah managed to wriggle her left hand free and dug her fingers into the bandage on his thigh.

He howled in pain, lunging forward to grab her wrist. His hand caught on the chain around her neck and she felt it snap.

The dove pendant landed on the pavement a few feet away.

The plane's engines roared to life.

"Get her in the plane, Tomas," the injured man yelled. He struggled to his feet, one hand holding his leg just above the blood-soaked bandage.

Tomas kicked her knife away and hauled her to her feet. Sarah struggled, but he was prepared this time. His hand only tightened on her arm as he dragged her up the stairs. Her side twinged in pain when she tried to yank out of his grip.

She'd probably torn her stitches. Again.

"Sarah!" The voice was in her earpiece, but Sarah looked up to see the other two SUVs entering the clearing. They approached fast, tires squealing on the cracked pavement.

It was too late.

Tomas pulled Sarah inside and she watched, helpless, as the injured man closed the door. The plane immediately started moving down the runway.

Tomas let go of her. She elbowed him in the face.

It wouldn't get her anywhere, but it sure felt good.

"Bitch!" the injured man snarled. He yanked her hands behind her back and tightened a plastic zip tie around her wrists, so tight she was sure it would cut off circulation.

Through the window, she saw Roman jump out of the SUV and lift a gun, firing several shots at the retreating jet. They pinged uselessly off the exterior.

The dove pendant - and the team's only way of tracking her - lay useless on the pavement.

The steady whirring of the plane's wheels on the concrete disappeared as it lifted into the air.

She was going to die.

The men patted her down. She tried to knee one of them in the groin, but they were catching on to her tricks. It didn't take them long to find her ankle holster. Tomas pulled out her Glock and admired it. "You won't need this where we're going."

"Sarah." Roman's voice was in her ear again, low and urgent. The static was worse the further away from him she got. His voice was barely understandable. "You stay alive, you hear me? Stay alive."

"Check for a wire," the injured man said.

Tomas smiled and reached for her shirt. Sarah jerked away from him. "Don't touch me. Get away from me!"

"I'll find you," Roman said. "I promise. I promise!"

Tomas yanked her shirt up, exposing bare skin, and with one swift yank, pulled out her wire. Sarah yelped when he pulled it out of her ear. He dropped the whole thing to the floor and, never taking his eyes from her face, crushed it underneath his boot.

"When Altez is finished with you, you'll wish we had killed your mother instead of taking you."

Sarah didn't respond. She couldn't pull her eyes away from the broken pieces of her wire, the last connection she had to the only people who could save her.

CHAPTER 16

"**DAMMIT!**" Emmett slammed his fist into the wall. It went through the sheetrock, leaving a huge hole in its wake. He shook the dust from his hand and began to pace, eyeing Owen. "You can't find anything?"

They were back at the ESI office, gathered in the briefing room. Everyone looked as defeated as Roman felt. He had replayed the scene in his mind a thousand times, looking for a way that he could've prevented Sarah from being taken.

Thinking in circles never got him anywhere.

With Mary safe at the La Conner hospital, Chance and Bellamy watching over her, it was the rest of the team's job to come up with a plan.

Owen sat at a table nearby with his laptop in front of him, face pale as he typed. His brow knitted into a frown. "I used satellite imagery to catch sight of them as they took off. I know they headed south, but they're flying low, in the clouds, and I lost them. That pilot knows how to avoid detection."

So in a nutshell, they had nothing. No way to track her, no leads to follow.

They were dead in the water.

If they didn't do something, soon Sarah would be dead too.

What did Altez want with her?

Roman thought he knew.

Altez wanted revenge for his wife's death, and what better way to make Roman pay than to torture and kill the woman Roman loved?

… Loved?

Oh damn.

He loved Sarah.

Roman swore under his breath. "I can't just sit here."

Nobody spoke as he stormed from the room, and nobody tried to stop him.

He left the building and went out back, where there was nothing but trees beyond, and took a deep breath. Sarah's words drifted back to him.

Thank you, for everything.

She knew.

Roman's hands clenched into fists. Somehow, Sarah knew she wouldn't make it back from the exchange, but she decided to play the hero anyway.

Who was he kidding?

Sarah didn't 'play' the hero. She was the bravest, most capable woman he'd ever met. Most of the men he'd served with wouldn't willingly give themselves over to an unknown enemy in order to save someone.

She was incredible.

She also had no idea what she'd gotten herself into.

Roman had been in Altez's organization long enough to know how he operated. There was a reason no one knew his true identity. No one made it out alive to tell the tale.

He couldn't let Sarah meet the same fate.

Roman pulled out his cell phone and scrolled through his contacts.

Jeffries had connections. He'd been keeping tabs on Altez for years. Maybe he could help them.

Roman put the phone to his ear and listened to it ring.

And ring. And ring.

Jeffries didn't answer.

"Damn it." Roman shoved the phone back into his pocket and leaned his head back against the wall.

"Roman."

He glanced over his shoulder. Emmett stood nearby, watching him.

Roman turned back to look at the trees.

Emmett stepped up beside him and followed his gaze. "This is Sarah's favorite thing to do when she's stressed. She stares at the trees like they have all the answers... a lot like what you're doing right now."

Roman's jaw tightened. "She shouldn't have been out there."

"I know."

"It should've been me. I'm the one Altez wants."

Emmett was silent for a moment. "I don't think we give Sarah enough credit. She handled that situation better than any member of this team could have."

"Yeah, but she shouldn't have to. She's not a member

of this team."

Emmett sighed. "I know. And that's part of the reason we're in this mess. Because I was too bull-headed to listen to her. But my mom's alive because of her quick thinking."

"She shouldn't have been in this situation in the first place. None of you should have been. I brought this trouble right to your doorstep."

"No. I knew what I was getting into when I recruited you."

Roman looked at him in surprise. "What?"

Emmett stared out into the trees. "I didn't meet you by chance - but you already knew that. Jeffries contacted me. He's the one who suggested that you would be a good fit for my team."

"Jeffries?"

"Yes. He didn't give me much information, just that you served your country well and you needed something to keep you occupied. I did some digging from there."

"You mean Owen did some digging."

"Of course." Emmett smiled briefly. "I knew you were in special forces, undercover for years, and that someone very powerful wanted your head." He paused. "We're not so different. I knew I needed you on my team."

"Someone wants your head?"

"Several someones."

Roman hesitated. This was a rare opportunity; Emmett was volunteering information about his past. What could he ask without Emmett shutting down?

"I know you have feelings for my sister." Emmett waited a moment, giving Roman ample time to deny it.

When he didn't, Emmett continued. "We'll get her back, but I need your head in the game. I'm worried too, but if we aren't one hundred percent focused, she'll die."

"I know."

"Good. She's lucky to have you in her corner." Emmett extended a hand.

Roman reached out and they gripped each other's forearms in a gesture of solidarity. "Thank you," he said quietly.

Dominick poked his head around the corner. "Hey, if you guys are done making love back here, Owen found something."

Emmett and Roman smiled a little at each other and followed Dominick inside.

"... Not in Spain like I thought," Owen was saying as they entered the room. His eyes met theirs. "I was able to decode the SD card. You'll never believe this. I know what Altez wanted from Ryan, and I know where Sarah is."

* * * * *

It felt like they were in the air forever.

The men - their names were Tomas and Manuel, she learned - kept the shades down over the windows. She couldn't even tell which direction they were flying in.

Not that it would've helped. She had no way to relay the information back to the team.

Sarah spent the flight strapped to a chair in the back of the plane. About two hours into the flight, she got Tomas's attention - he was the uninjured one - and showed him her hands. They were purple. Grudgingly, he took off the zip tie and bound her hands in front of her, a little looser this time to allow some blood flow.

Tomas and Manuel sat toward the front of the plane and alternated between arguing loudly in Spanish and looking generally mean.

Sarah listened to them talk, wishing for the hundredth time that she'd paid attention in high school Spanish. Too bad she had spent more time drooling over boys than paying attention.

If it didn't involve asking where the bathroom was, she couldn't understand it.

"Hey," she called. "Mind telling me where we're going?"

Manuel glowered at her. "Shut up."

Sarah sat back against her seat and waited until they went back to their conversation. Her head pounded something fierce, and her side had been aching for hours. Gingerly, she used her bound hands to inch her shirt up so she could examine her wound.

Sure enough, the Ace bandage wrapped around her midsection was soaked red.

Again.

Sarah let out a disgusted breath and looked up to see Manuel standing a few feet away. He was staring at the bare skin of her stomach.

She dropped her shirt back down and glared at him. "Got a problem?"

"Tomas," he called. "Her wound is bleeding. Come here and hold her."

"Don't touch me. My wound is fine."

Tomas shouldered past Manuel and grabbed her hands. He lifted them above her head and held them firmly in place. Sarah struggled, but she was helpless as Manuel advanced.

"Altez won't be happy if you die before he can meet you," Manuel murmured. His fingers grasped her shirt and he yanked it up above her chest.

Sarah let out an outraged scream and renewed her struggles. Thank God she had worn a sports bra. It didn't seem to deter Manuel, though. He looked down at her like a lion looked at a gazelle.

His fingers touched her bare skin. They were like ice.

Sarah jerked away from him. "Get off me!"

"Manuel," Tomas said from behind her. "Altez was clear on his instructions. Change her bandage."

Manuel growled low in his throat and shot Tomas an annoyed glance, but he swiftly unwound her bandage. She felt him spread something cold across her wound and almost cried in relief when the pain immediately started ebbing away.

"W-What is that?" she demanded.

Manuel didn't answer, but instead wrapped a new bandage around her stomach. His fingers lingered against her bare skin and began slowly tracing upward over her bra.

When his hands slipped underneath it, Sarah roared in outrage and bucked. She threw her head forward and slammed it against his.

Manuel stumbled back, dazed from the blow, and fell into the opposite seat. Sarah lifted a booted foot and kicked him in the injured leg. He roared in pain and surged up, his face contorted into a mask of fury, his dark skin mottled with red.

Sarah tried to wriggle away, but he advanced too quickly and his hands circled her neck.

And he squeezed.

Tomas dropped her hands, yelling in Spanish at Manuel.

Sarah grabbed his wrists, trying desperately to loosen his grip. She couldn't breathe. She couldn't think. All she could do was stare into his dark, furious eyes while he killed her.

Just when the edges of her vision began to turn black, Tomas grabbed Manuel's arm and hauled him away from her.

Sarah leaned forward, coughing and breathing deep gulps of air, and thanked God that she wasn't dead.

Yet.

"No hands on her," Tomas snapped. "You heard Altez."

Manuel glared at Sarah. "That bitch attacked me."

"I don't care. We follow Altez's orders."

The two men glowered at each other for a moment, then Manuel finally relented. "Put her out. I don't want any more trouble," he snarled as he walked back to the front of the plane.

Tomas muttered angrily to himself in Spanish and reached into a black bag a few seats up. Sarah watched as he uncapped a needle, horror growing with every passing second.

Roman's words echoed in her mind.

Stay alive.

She shrank away from Tomas when he approached, but there was nowhere to go. He grabbed her arm and sank the needle into it with one fluid movement.

Sarah jerked away, but it was too late. "What is that? What did you do?"

Her vision blurred. Her thoughts began to collide and run together. She couldn't get her body to do what she wanted, and she thought she might've screamed, but she wasn't sure.

Everything went black.

CHAPTER 17

THE PLANE JOLTED as its wheels hit the ground.

Sarah jerked her head up, then immediately regretted it. A wave of dizziness had her stomach rolling. In a panic, she looked around for something to vomit into. When she saw nothing, she took a few deep breaths, praying silently that her stomach would settle.

Tomas and Manuel bustled around the plane as it came to a stop. The door opened and blinding sunlight flooded the cabin.

Sarah squeezed her eyes shut against stabbing pain and groaned. A jolt of pain shot through her throat at the sound and she winced.

What was going on? Why did she feel like she was hit by a truck?

Oh, right. Tomas and the needle. What had he injected into her system?

Whatever it was, she hoped it wouldn't do any lasting damage.

Sarah opened her eyes at the sound of footsteps.

Tomas was approaching her. Manuel limped down the stairs at the front of the plane, cursing under his breath, one hand pressed to the bandage around his leg.

Served him right.

Tomas hauled her to her feet. Sarah stumbled against him. Her legs still weren't obeying her brain. She shook her head against another bout of dizziness and commanded herself to stay alert.

"Not so chatty now, are you?" Tomas laughed and yanked her forward.

He led her out of the plane and down the steps. Sarah was assaulted by a wall of heavy, humid heat and it took her a moment to remember how to breathe. As Tomas herded her across the runway, she blinked against the bright sunlight, trying to survey her surroundings.

Forest surrounded them on all sides, but the trees were strange. There were no evergreen trees like she had back home.

No, it wasn't a forest.

It was a jungle.

They were in the jungle.

Sarah stumbled again, this time in shock, and Tomas muttered irritably as he dragged her to a waiting jeep. It was green, rusted, and smelled like sweat and blood. Tomas threw her inside and shut the door. Then he climbed into the passenger seat up front next to Manuel.

The jeep took off at an unsafe speed.

Sarah bumped around in the back seat and tried to use her bound hands to push herself into a sitting position. The road was riddled with potholes and divots, and Manuel was driving like a bat out of hell. If she didn't sit up so she could see out the window, she was going to throw up all over the seat.

She tried to call out to them, tell them to slow down, but her throat hurt too badly. Her voice was gone. Instead, she settled back against the seat and closed her eyes, trying to take deep breaths against the disgusting smells wafting up from the cracked leather.

They drove along that terrible road for what felt like hours. Sarah tried the door latch, hoping to throw herself out of the vehicle and make a run for it, but the men were smart enough to engage the childproof locks.

She needed a plan, some kind of strategy to keep herself alive.

But even if she could escape, where was she? How would she get home?

She didn't think they were in the United States anymore. A white girl in a foreign jungle didn't have a snowball's chance in Hell of surviving.

Stay alive.

How was she going to do that? They hadn't blindfolded her, so they obviously didn't intend to let her go. She wouldn't make it out alive to identify where she'd been kept.

Her odds didn't look good.

After what felt like an eternity, the road finally smoothed out - if you could call gravel smooth - and the jungle around them began to thin. Before long, they rattled to a stop. Sarah strained to look out the window.

They were parked in front of a massive cement wall

that must have been fifteen feet high. A wrought-iron gate stood in front of them, with armed guards standing on either side. They wore faded camo clothing and brandished automatic rifles.

Manuel exchanged a few words with them in Spanish and they opened the gate, leering at her as the jeep passed through.

Sarah examined their surroundings, trying to memorize anything that might be important. A cluster of small buildings sat just inside the wall. It looked like a village that stretched a couple acres, if she had to guess. The buildings were small and poorly constructed. A couple looked like they might fall over at any moment. The most well-built structures around were the large towers built into the cement wall. She could see one from her vantage point, and if she squinted hard enough, she thought she could see men standing in the open top of it.

People milled around, watching their vehicle as it drove past. They were all men, dressed in plain clothing, but every single one had a gun.

Sarah shrank away from the window and kept her head down. Something was eerily familiar about this place. If her mind wasn't so fuzzy, she would have known right away. But it took her a few minutes to figure it out.

Then it dawned on her.

This looked like the same compound that ESI had investigated a week ago.

Sarah peeked out the window again. The more she looked, the more sure she became.

What had Owen said about it?

Armed to the teeth, too dangerous to infiltrate.

She was so screwed.

The jeep rattled up to the main building that stood in the center of the village. It was a mansion, built like the ones she'd seen in California, with white stucco walls and an exotic-looking red shingled roof. It stuck out like a sore thumb compared to the bare adobe buildings surrounding it.

A second gate opened and the jeep entered a beautifully manicured courtyard, where it finally came to a complete stop. Manuel and Tomas got out, and Tomas dragged Sarah out of the back seat. Manuel hobbled along beside them as they entered the mansion. The floor was covered in ornate tile and Sarah stared in awe at the magnificent chandelier hanging in the entryway. Armed guards were everywhere, observing them in stony silence.

One guard stepped away from a nearby wall and conversed in terse tones with Tomas. He turned and led them to the right, down a wide hallway. He opened a door and gestured them inside. It was an office, the most beautiful Sarah had ever seen. The ceiling was tall and bookcases lined three walls. The fourth wall was one large window overlooking the fountain in the courtyard. A massive desk dominated the middle of the room. It was freshly polished and smelled like lemons.

The chair behind the desk was leather, with a tall back, and it was facing away from her. Once the door shut behind them, the chair swung around.

Like a cheesy villain in a Disney movie, Altez revealed himself.

He was a handsome man, dark-complexioned, with

dark eyes and perfectly slicked-back black hair. His features were the kind of perfect that could only be achieved by a surgeon's knife. When he stood, he didn't appear that tall, but his teeth were perfectly white and straight as he smiled and spread his arms wide.

"Welcome to my home," he said warmly. "I am so pleased to meet you."

Sarah didn't answer. She couldn't even if she wanted to.

"I am Arturo Montez. I am so happy you're here, Sarah Erickson."

Arturo Montez... Owen was right! Maybe there was a chance the team would find her after all.

Arturo came around his desk and stopped when he was only a few feet away from her. His eyes swept over her face and down to her toes, then back up again.

"Manuel, what happened to my guest's neck?" Arturo's voice was pleasant, silky smooth, and his smile didn't slip as he continued to look at Sarah.

Manuel shifted behind her. "She attacked me, *dominar*," he said.

Arturo smiled, and a shiver slid down Sarah's spine. It wasn't a pleasant smile, even though his expression was friendly. "Were my instructions unclear?"

"No, *dominar*."

"No. You are correct."

Faster than Sarah could react, a small handgun appeared in Arturo's hand. The shot was deafening in the office; Sarah jumped at the sudden noise. She kept her eyes on Arturo, willing herself not to scream as she heard

Manuel's lifeless body topple to the floor.

"Please take the garbage out before it stains my rug." Arturo's voice was as pleasant as ever. He turned his gaze back to her as a couple of men dragged Manuel's body out of the office. "Please, sit. We have much to discuss."

Sarah sat. She watched numbly as Arturo returned to his chair on the other side of the desk. He steepled his fingers and watched her over the top of them.

"I apologize for the display. As you can see, I cannot employ one who is not able to follow orders." He looked almost sad. "It's unfortunate. I did like Manuel. I was very fond of Ryan, too. He has been a wonderful asset as of late."

How dare he speak about Ryan. Sarah wanted to scream, rage, dive across the table, but Roman's words echoed in her mind again.

Stay alive.

"He would have been a wonderful doctor someday. It's unfortunate that he couldn't follow orders either."

"You..." Sarah's voice was barely audible. She cleared her throat painfully and tried again. "You killed him."

"Yes." Arturo regarded her thoughtfully. "You're very beautiful, Sarah. Your photos don't do you justice."

The look in his eyes made her want to scrub herself all over with hot soap.

Arturo tore his gaze from hers and looked to someone behind her. "Please show Miss Erickson to her bedroom. Provide her with some tea to soothe her throat." When he met her eyes again, his not-truly-pleasant smile was back. "I'll provide some clothes for you to wear. Please join me for dinner this evening. We have much to discuss, but I'm sure you'd like to rest first." He paused, and his smile widened just slightly. "And please, wear your hair down tonight. It's a shame to keep it pulled back."

CHAPTER 18

THE ROAR OF THE JET'S ENGINES drowned out almost all other sound. Roman disassembled his SIG for the fifth time and put it back together, trying in vain to keep his mind blank and focused on the mission.

Around him, the rest of the team sat silently. Even Owen had come along for this. He sat in the back of the plane with his laptop open on his lap.

The air was thick with tension.

Sarah had been missing for almost 24 hours.

The unspoken question hung in the air. Was she even still alive?

She was. Roman had to believe it, or he'd go batshit crazy.

A door swung open from the front of the plane and Emmett stepped out of the cockpit. He, like everyone else, was dressed in black tactical pants and a black t-shirt. His belt was loaded with two holsters, a utility knife, and a taser.

"ETA twenty minutes," he announced to the group. "Load up."

Nobody voiced a response, but a flurry of activity ensued as they loaded their weapons and placed them in strategic positions on their bodies.

Roman had been ready since they took off, so he remained seated and stared out the window as the jet began its descent.

Owen remained glued to his laptop, his face unnaturally pale as he typed away.

Roman watched him for a moment, then sighed and made his way to the back of the plane.

Owen didn't look up as Roman dropped into the seat next to him.

"You all right?"

"Just peachy." Owen's voice was strained. His fingers tapped even faster on the keyboard, if that was possible. "My sister is in the hands of a psychopath and the last interaction we had was when I betrayed her trust. So thanks, I'm just dandy."

"We'll get her out."

Owen finally looked up. His green eyes were sharp. "Don't make promises you can't keep, Holt. I've read this guy's dossier. I'm aware of the likelihood that she's already dead."

"She's not dead. Altez won't kill her so quickly."

Owen groaned and slumped down in his seat. "Is that supposed to be comforting? Jeez, I could use a vacation. Why am I not in the Bahamas right now? Psychotic murderers don't go to the Bahamas."

Roman rested a hand on Owen's shoulder. "Sarah can kick the shit out of anyone in her way. She'll be fine. By the time we get there, Altez and his crew will probably be dead and Sarah will be drinking margaritas on the pile of their dead bodies."

Owen let out a choked laugh. "I'm never going to get that image out of my head."

Emmett walked down the aisle, stopping next to them. "Ready?"

Roman and Owen nodded.

"You get a hold of Jeffries yet?"

"No." Roman ran a hand over his hair, clasping the back of his neck. "He's not answering his phone. Even if he did, though, his hands are tied."

Emmett nodded. "Same response from my contacts. This is a shitty situation. Uncle Sam won't authorize any teams to converge on the area because of the risk. We're on our own."

Roman didn't answer. His stomach was churning too much to come up with an answer.

"ESI can handle it," Owen said, shooting Roman a look. "And Sarah can handle herself. We've got this."

Emmett cracked a small smile and returned to the front of the cabin where he could see everyone.

"Listen up," he said. His voice wasn't loud, but the authority was so clear that everyone immediately stilled and turned their attention to him. "We're outmanned and outgunned on this, and backup won't be coming. Altez's compound is heavily fortified. We stick with our original extraction plan. Everyone clear?"

There were general grunts and exclamations of agreement. Roman looked around at his team. Would any of them make it out of this alive? He felt a rush of gratitude for these men who would risk their lives for Sarah. He saw no hesitation in their eyes as they listened to Emmett go over the plan again.

If anyone could pull this off, it was ESI.

As the ground approached, the pilot killed the lights and the jet landed without incident. The ramp at the back of the jet opened, its mechanical screeching loud in the approaching darkness. The team crouched low, guns up, and exited the plane. They paused in a defensive position and listened, scanning the area with their night vision goggles.

Silence.

Roman looked to Emmett, who nodded back at him. "Go time," he said quietly into their comms.

* * * * *

Tomas took Sarah to a bedroom on the second floor of the mansion. He opened the door and shoved her inside. "I'll be back to get you for dinner," he snapped, and closed the door behind her. She heard the 'snick' of the lock engaging on the other side.

Rubbing her arm where he'd gripped it, Sarah looked around the room. It was as lavish as the rest of the house, with a giant king bed and spotless, plush white carpet.

Laid out across the bedspread was a magnificent green gown.

Sarah approached it cautiously and held it up. It was beautiful, made of satin, floor-length with one strap and a line of emeralds sewn into the belt.

It looked to be exactly her size.

Sarah shivered. How had Arturo known her size? Actually, she didn't want to know. The thought creeped her out too much to dwell on.

She ignored the dress and looked around the room for anything she could use as a weapon, but there was nothing. She tried the window, but it was latched shut and she couldn't find a way to open it.

Nowhere to go. Nothing to use to defend herself.

As a few minutes passed, Sarah remembered how quickly Arturo had drawn that gun on Manuel. The thought spurred her to action. If she couldn't escape now, she'd have to play by Arturo's rules, or risk getting herself shot.

She opened another door and entered an elegant bathroom. Everything she needed was provided for her, including shampoo and conditioner, a razor - the cheap disposable kind, not one she could use to fight with -, and new bandages for her gunshot wound.

Sarah showered quickly and dried her hair. There was makeup in a silk bag on the counter, so she applied some blush and mascara. She didn't necessarily want to look pretty for Arturo, but he might shoot her if she didn't make an attempt.

Sarah paused to look at herself in the mirror and frowned. No wonder Arturo had been so angry with Manuel. Even with Sarah's hair falling in waves down her back, the dark purple bruises in the shape of handprints on her neck stood out against her pale skin.

Carefully, Sarah put a finger to one and pressed lightly.

The twinge of pain she received confirmed that the bruises were deep. She'd probably suffered swelling to her vocal chords and that's why she was having trouble speaking.

Sarah stared at her reflection for a moment longer, looking into her own dark green eyes. "You will make it through this," she told herself. "You have to believe that. You have to survive."

The echo of Roman's words caused goosebumps to break out across her skin.

Someone pounded on the bedroom door.

Her time was up.

Sarah shimmied into the green gown. The fabric was soft on her freshly-washed skin. If this was any other time, she would revel in the feeling. A pair of glittery black heels sat on the floor next to the bed. Just like the dress, they fit her perfectly.

The door slammed open and Tomas gestured at her, obviously irritated that she'd made him wait. Sarah followed him down the hallway and back downstairs, where he showed her to the dining room. The sun was beginning to set outside, casting an orange glow across the room.

Like the rest of the mansion, the dining room was decorated elegantly. The dining table was long enough to seat at least fifty people, and covered with a white tablecloth. The chairs looked hand-carved with ornate backs. Candlelight from the candelabra on the table flickered, casting shadows across the polished china.

Arturo sat at the head of the table. A man she didn't recognize sat beside him. Judging from his sandy blond hair and blue eyes, he wasn't one of Arturo's flunkies.

They both rose when she entered, and Arturo's gaze took in her figure, appreciation evident in his expression.

Sarah tried to keep her smile pleasant as revulsion slithered down her spine.

"Ah, darling. You look breathtaking. I knew that dress would look wonderful on you."

Sarah nodded her thanks and waited for Arturo to pull out her chair. When she sat, his hands settled on her bare shoulders and lingered there. His skin was warm, but she felt cold where he touched her. She stiffened and waited until he finally released her and sat down before she took another breath.

Arturo smiled at her as he returned to his chair. Only then did he gesture to the man beside him. "This is Michael Jeffries. He's an associate of mine, visiting with us for the week."

Sarah's eyes narrowed. She took in the man's muscled frame, the shadows in his eyes.

It couldn't be.

"Jeffries?" she asked.

Jeffries nodded, his pleasant smile never faltering.

Sarah glanced between him and Arturo. What was going on here?

"Yes, this is the Jeffries you think it is." Arturo's smile was pleasant. "He's been in my employ for years now."

Sarah's stomach dropped.

No. Roman's team lead…

He would be crushed if he found out.

Arturo made a small gesture with one hand. Out of nowhere, men dressed in tuxedos appeared and set plates in front of them. "You must be hungry. It's been a terribly long day for you. Please, eat."

Sarah looked down at her plate. It was a salad, bright green and artfully arranged. Her stomach growled, but she didn't pick up her fork. She glanced at Arturo, who was watching her.

He chuckled. "Don't worry, it's not poisoned. See?" He speared some lettuce on her plate with his fork and placed it in his mouth. He made a show of chewing and swallowing for her benefit.

Sarah felt only minorly relieved, but she cautiously took a bite.

Dammit, it was delicious.

Arturo smiled and began eating as well. "I must thank you," he said between bites, "for bringing me the SD card."

"I didn't have much of a choice." Her voice was raspy, but it was returning.

He smiled in acknowledgment.

Did the man ever stop smiling? It was creepy.

"How much did Ryan tell you about his responsibilities?"

"Nothing." Sarah glanced at Jeffries. He ate his meal in silence, his eyes never leaving his plate.

"Oh, come now. There's no reason for us to lie to each other, my dear."

"I'm not. Ryan never told me what he did. I didn't even know he had a job."

"Oh, he did." Arturo continued to smile.

Sarah wanted to smack it right off his smug face.

"He was supplying very important information to me. Because of the information on that SD card, I won't have to worry about anything for the rest of my life."

"What information is that?" Sarah pretended disinterest, picking at the last few pieces of lettuce on her plate.

"You're his roommate. You had the SD card. You don't know what's on it?" Arturo's voice was pleasant, but Sarah sensed he didn't believe her.

"It's encrypted. I couldn't open it."

"Ah." Arturo waved a hand and their plates were taken away, quickly replaced by the main course. Juicy-looking steak, vegetables, and steaming mashed potatoes. "I am glad I've treated you so kindly, then. I treated Ryan kindly as well, though I knew he would someday betray me."

"Betray you?"

"Of course. I took that chance when I recruited the mole's brother."

Sarah's blood turned to ice. She prayed her sudden terror didn't show in her expression. "M-Mole?"

"Ah, dear girl." Arturo gave her a pitying look. "Don't play dumb with me. It's not becoming. I know you are close with Roman, just as I knew he was a mole from the beginning. My sources don't fail me."

Sarah kept her eyes on her plate. Jeffries had been reporting to Arturo from the beginning. That meant none of the information Roman reported was true. His entire operation had been doomed from the beginning.

He raised his glass to Jeffries, then lifted a piece of steak for her to see. It was cooked rare, and red droplets fell from his fork. "Even though I knew he would betray me, I couldn't stop him from murdering Maria."

Arturo reached across the table and caressed the back of Sarah's left hand. She jerked it out of his reach and rested it in her lap.

"My wife. Roman murdered her in cold blood. Jeffries here warned me about the raid on my compound, but he was new to my ranks. None of my other sources reported the chatter, so I didn't believe him. By pure luck, I happened to be held up on a deal out of town that night. Roman's team raided my home and killed my Maria while I wasn't there." Arturo paused. His dark eyes were emotionless, despite talking about the death of his wife. It was creepy. "You look so much like her, you know. She had beautiful blonde hair like yours."

The food in Sarah's stomach turned sour.

"Since he stole the love of my life, it's only fair that I steal his." Arturo smiled pleasantly. "So I hired his brother. I figured I could kill him to send the message to Roman that he never should have betrayed me. But Roman never contacted his brother. Poor Ryan was so heartbroken that his brother abandoned him." Arturo's expression turned mournful. "He turned out to be quite useful, so I kept him on the payroll. Until he betrayed me, just like his brother did."

Sarah saw red. The anguished look in Roman's eyes when he talked about Ryan. The pain she felt as she watched the last breath escape Ryan's lips. Tom's lifeless body lying in his bedroom.

Every moment of sadness and heartbreak since Arturo had intruded on her life.

No, even before that, when her father died after a long

battle with cancer.

So much death. So much pain.

And Arturo felt no guilt for his part in it.

Stay alive.

He was evil, and he would continue to hurt innocent people. People she loved.

If she didn't act now, she'd never get another chance to do something about it.

Sarah surged to her feet. Her fingers curled around the steak knife lying across her plate. Before anyone could react, she plunged the blade through Arturo's hand and into the solid wood dining table.

Arturo let out an inhuman screech.

His guards rushed forward. Hands closed around Sarah's arms and yanked her away from the table. She fought madly to break their grip, but they each had a hundred pounds on her.

Jeffries gripped the knife handle and yanked it out of his boss's hand. Arturo screamed again and cradled the bloody appendage to his chest.

He looked up, and Sarah saw death in his eyes.

"Get. Her. Out of here!" he snarled.

Sarah struggled with all her might and managed to elbow one of the men in the nose. She didn't stop to look, but she hoped it was Tomas again. His grip loosened and she turned to knee the other guard in the groin. He dropped like a rock.

Free!

Sarah turned to flee, but she forgot she was wearing heels. Her right ankle rolled when she took her first step, and she was tackled from behind before she could recover.

She felt more than heard a loud crack.

She screamed in pain, but her throat was still too swollen. The only sound she made was a hoarse shout.

Arturo was still yelling, but he had switched to Spanish. The unfamiliar words rolled over her head as she curled up into a ball, scrabbling to reach her wounded ankle.

Jeffries grabbed her arm and hauled her to her feet. He was the one who had tackled her. Her ankle dragged along the floor as he pulled her away, sending a massive jolt up her leg with each step. Her vision went black, so all she could see was a pinprick of light.

As Jeffries dragged her through the doorway, she saw Arturo still cradling his bleeding hand and felt a vicious surge of satisfaction. "Better stop the bleeding before your precious master bleeds out," she yelled.

It didn't sound as intimidating as she would've liked, because her voice broke from the effort.

Instead of taking her upstairs and back to her bedroom, Jeffries instead opened a door that led to a basement. This space was opposite of the rest of the mansion. The steps were stone and dirty. The air turned cool, then cold, as they descended into the darkness.

Sarah tried to remain conscious so she could remember the route back to the main house.

As if she had a prayer of escaping at this point.

"You were Roman's friend," she said, looking up at Jeffries. "Why would you work for someone like Altez?"

Jeffries shrugged. "I was in the forces a long time. They don't pay nearly enough for the amount of shit I dealt with.

Arturo had a better offer."

"But all the innocent people..."

Jeffries led her down a long, narrow hallway that angled down until they reached an honest-to-God prison cell.

"People die every day." His voice was cold, and his grip didn't loosen as he unlocked the metal door. "Might as well get paid."

He threw her inside.

Sarah landed in a heap and bit back another scream when it jarred her ankle.

"Roman will come for me," she said. "And you don't want to be here when he does."

Jeffries paused outside her cell. "Help isn't coming, princess. Roman will be dead before he reaches this compound."

Jeffries' footsteps echoed back to her as he returned to the surface.

When all was quiet, she hauled herself into a sitting position. It was too dark to see her ankle. The only light source was down the hallway, nowhere hear her cell.

Gingerly, she ran her fingers down her leg, gritting her teeth against the pain. The bone wasn't protruding from her skin, so that was good, but she was pretty sure it was broken.

Her breath shuddered out of her and she pulled her good knee up to her chest, resting her forehead on it.

Jeffries was working for Arturo.

Everything finally clicked into place.

He was friends with Roman, so he had access to turn

Ryan. He knew every step Roman took.

Arturo was *playing* with Roman.

Sarah was probably another pawn in Arturo's vendetta. He would use her to hurt Roman.

She couldn't stop him.

A few minutes later, footsteps echoed down the hall again. Sarah pushed herself back against the wall, as far away from the door as she could get, and braced herself.

She saw the bouncing light of a flashlight first, then Tomas's face appeared in front of the door. "You will regret your actions this day," he said in a low voice.

In the light of the flashlight, she could see that his nose was crooked and rapidly swelling.

So it *was* him that she elbowed in the face.

If Owen was here, he would joke that she'd scored extra points.

"Maybe," Sarah whispered painfully. "But I won't regret stabbing your boss."

Tomas's face twisted into a sneer. "If you think you will receive a quick death, you are wrong. Altez is never merciful."

Sarah stared at him in stony silence.

After a moment, Tomas grunted in disgust and walked away, back to the surface.

Sarah laid down on her side and curled into herself. Tears leaked down her cheeks.

Was this how she was going to die?

CHAPTER 19

ROMAN CROUCHED IN THE BUSHES twenty yards away from the outer walls of Altez's compound. Emmett, Owen, and Chance huddled next to him. They blended into the jungle, silent and watchful as they waited for Emmett's signal to proceed.

Dominick and Cameron had already disappeared. Dominick took his place high in a tree with a view of the entire compound, so he could provide cover fire. Cameron had set explosives nearby where Roman was crouched, and now he was assigned to set explosives on the other side of the compound so they could attack on two fronts.

Roman took deep, quiet breaths to steady his erratic pulse. He kept his eyes on Emmett and every muscle tensed when Emmett glanced at his watch.

Chance and Owen crouched nearby. For all his technological knowledge, Owen was also experienced in the field. His calm expression and the steady hands on his rifle were a clear indication that his head was in the game, not distracted by the thought of his twin's well-being.

Dammit, Roman needed to snap out of it.

Emmett signaled at Chance, who nodded once and disappeared into the jungle, en route to meet up with Cameron at the other entry point.

Thirty seconds.

Roman raised his gun, sent a silent prayer to anyone who might be listening, and looked toward the compound.

The boom of multiple detonations shook the ground. Immediately, panicked shouts rose up from inside the wall. Roman, Emmett, and Owen ran silently through the dust and into the newly-formed hole in the cement wall. Roman heard the distant "pop" of gunfire, but he didn't know if it was coming from his team or the enemy's.

No suppressors this time.

He came up behind two men standing near the closest building. His knife entered one man's throat and he dropped without a sound. The other man turned, bringing his gun up to fire, but Roman yanked it out of his hands and knocked him out with a swift right hook. Over his shoulder, he observed that Owen and Emmett had already taken out the rest of the nearby guards.

He and Owen skirted the wall of the building, ignoring terrified workers as they ran for cover. There were no shots fired from the guard towers above, which meant that Dominick was doing his job and keeping them busy.

Emmett took the lead as they made their way up the dusty road and to the main building. For how heavily armed the compound was, they didn't meet much resistance. Most of Altez's men seemed to be either poorly lacking in skill or else running scared at the invasion.

Clearly, Altez had never planned for someone to infiltrate his compound.

He was as arrogant as ever.

It would be his downfall.

ESI worked flawlessly as a team. Owen followed closely behind Emmett and provided cover fire as they made their way through enemy territory. Roman brought up the rear and watched their backs, eyes alert for any sign of an ambush.

"Back wall is clear," Chance reported in Roman's earpiece.

"Any casualties?" Emmett's voice echoed in front of him and in his comm.

"Negative."

"Good. Secure the perimeter. We're entering the house now."

"Roger."

Emmett gestured over his shoulder. Owen and Roman stuck close on his heels as they ran toward the house. There was no movement in any of the windows, no spatter of gunfire as they approached.

The hairs on the back of Roman's neck stood up.

Something wasn't right.

* * * * *

The dim "boom" shook the ground in Sarah's cell. Dust and small rocks rained down from the ceiling. Sarah covered her head and rolled under the small cot in the corner, praying that the whole building wouldn't come down around her ears. Distant shouting echoed down to her and she struggled to her elbows.

That didn't sound planned.

Had Roman come to her rescue?

The thought filled her with so much hope and terror that she was suddenly dizzy. She dragged herself out from under the bed and staggered to her feet. Any pressure on her foot caused unbearable agony, so she hopped over to the door using one hand on the cool stone wall for support. She looked down the hallway and cocked her head, listening.

She thought she heard gunfire. More shouts. Running feet?

Hurried footsteps echoed down the hallway to her cell. "Roman?" she croaked. He'd never find her in this maze. She cleared her throat and tried again. "Roman? Roman! I'm over here!"

The footsteps picked up their pace and Sarah sagged against the iron bars in relief.

But it wasn't Roman who had come to save her.

It was Arturo.

He was still dressed in his black suit from dinner, but he no longer wore the smoothly sinister expression that she'd begun to associate with him. He looked furious. His hand was wrapped in a clean, white bandage. They'd managed to stop the bleeding.

Too bad.

"No one is coming to rescue you," he snarled. Sarah jumped back from the door as he unlocked it and threw it open. "Come with me."

His guards weren't with him. If Sarah was at a hundred percent, she could take him down. But she wasn't; she couldn't even walk.

"No," she said.

Arturo's dark skin went white. His eyes looked black in the dim light as they narrowed on her. He didn't say anything else, merely stepped forward and aimed a sharp kick at her injured foot. Sarah tried to dodge but she wasn't fast enough. His blow landed on her ankle and she bit off a scream.

Her knees buckled. She collapsed to her hands and knees. The stone floor bit into the skin of her palms.

Arturo grabbed a fistful of her hair and yanked her head up to look at him. A knife was suddenly in his other hand; the metal glinted wickedly at her in the dim cell. He placed the blade to her neck and pressed just hard enough for the tip to break her skin.

A warm drop of blood trickled down her neck.

Sarah stared into Arturo's eyes, too terrified to breathe, let alone move.

"Come with me," Arturo said again. It wasn't a request. He kept his fist firmly in her hair and dragged Sarah out of the cell and up the hallway toward the stairs.

Each step was agony.

Sarah breathed in short bursts through her nose, fighting the urge to throw up.

They ascended the stairs and Arturo threw open the door to utter chaos. Men with huge machine guns ran to and fro, shouting orders to one another in Spanish. The unmistakable sound of gunfire erupted from outside in short bursts.

Tomas ran up to them, gun in hand. "The chopper is ready."

Arturo nodded and yanked Sarah close to him. "Come," he snapped.

They went up two more sets of stairs - the pain was almost more than Sarah could take - and wove their way through the men running in the direction of the front door.

Finally, Tomas opened a door that led to the roof and a waiting helicopter. Two more men guarded the vehicle, guns up and ready to defend their boss's escape. Tomas climbed into the pilot's seat and Arturo threw Sarah into the back. She landed hard and scrambled away from him as he climbed in beside her.

He grabbed her wrist and dragged her back until she sat on the chair right next to him.

"I won't let him take you," he yelled as the engines started up.

* * * * *

Roman's team breached the main house, guns up and ready to fire.

It was silent.

No guards, no servants, no running feet.

"Spread out," Emmett said. "Clear the house. If Sarah's here, I want her located."

Owen and Roman nodded.

Roman took the stairs directly in front of them, while Emmett headed to the right and Owen went left.

Roman cleared room by room, but the house was empty.

Was he too late?

When he reached the end of the hall, there was one door left.

Roman kicked it open and stepped inside, swinging his AK in a wide arc.

A man stood in the center of the room with a gun aimed at Roman's chest.

Roman froze. His finger hesitated on the trigger.

"Jeffries?"

His former team lead bobbed his head in acknowledgment. "I wish you hadn't come here, Holt."

"What are you--?" Roman stopped when Jeffries put his eye to the gun's sights.

Then it all clicked into place.

"Traitor."

"Yeah, yeah, I've heard it all before. Your little girlfriend told me." Jeffries' expression was cold. He looked like a different man than the one who led Roman's team for years.

"Where is she?"

"Sarah?" Jeffries paused, raising a finger to point at the ceiling. "You hear that?"

The tell-tale whirring of helicopter rotors sounded above them.

"Looks like she's making her exit." Jeffries smiled. "Unfortunately, you won't be joining her."

He raised his gun and pulled the trigger.

Roman dove out the door and into the hallway, but he couldn't outrun the bullet. It pierced his right side, just inside the fatty part of his skin.

He landed hard and rolled, coming up in a crouch.

"Shit." He pressed the button on his comms. "Emmett, I'm hit. Sarah's on the roof. Altez is taking her in a chopper."

"Roger." The sound of gunfire peppered the line. "I'll be there in a minute."

Roman ignored the pain in his side and ducked into the next room, using the wall for cover.

Moments later, Jeffries' footsteps sounded in the hall outside.

"Come out, come out, wherever you are."

Roman gritted his teeth. He didn't have time to play games with this asshole. If he didn't move fast, Sarah would be gone to him forever.

He couldn't let Altez take her.

He'd promised she would make it out.

Roman took a deep breath, centered himself, and rolled out into the hallway.

Jeffries didn't expect him to take such a direct approach. He was standing less than a foot away from the open doorway.

Roman came up firing, and his aim rang true.

Five bullets in the chest and his old friend went down.

"I'm on my way to the roof," Emmett said in his earpiece. "I've got Owen with me."

Roman had a million questions, but no time to ask them. He took one last look at his old leader's body.

Jeffries met his eyes, and his expression wasn't apologetic or sad. He didn't regret the decisions he'd made.

Roman would never know why Jeffries betrayed his country, and frankly, right now he didn't care.

Sarah was his one and only priority.

Roman touched his earpiece as he ran down the hallway. "Roger. I'm on my way too."

He left Jeffries lying there in his own blood and headed for the roof to save the love of his life.

* * * * *

The giant propeller above them began to turn, beating the air. The roar was so loud that Sarah almost couldn't make out Arturo's words. His hand went to her hair again and she flinched, but he only smoothed the blond strands.

Now that they were making their escape, his smile was pleasant and unruffled once again. "I have much planned for you, my dear."

Sarah jerked her head away from him.

Arturo merely smiled. His fingers wrapped around her arm in a bruising grip, holding her in place so she couldn't scoot away.

The helicopter's roar grew in intensity until she felt a jolt as it lifted into the air. Sarah whipped around to look out the window as they took off.

For the second time in 24 hours, she would watch as ESI tried to save her, but they were too late.

The door to the roof flew open. A figure rolled out onto the surface and came up firing. The two guards standing on the edge went down, their bodies falling to the ground below.

Roman. She would know him anywhere.

Roman's head turned toward the helicopter. He started running like he was going to try to catch it.

Arturo saw him too. He let go of Sarah and pulled a handgun from his belt. The helicopter door slid open easily. He leaned out and pointed his gun at Roman.

"No!" Sarah screamed. She threw herself at Arturo from behind just as he pulled the trigger.

Wow, she was getting really good at tackling people in the act of shooting the ones she loved.

The sound of the gunshot was almost drowned out by the sound of the helicopter's propeller.

Arturo's shot went wide. It hit the roof a few feet to the right of Roman. Sarah knew because she saw the sparks as it collided with the concrete.

Roman dove the other direction and rolled behind what looked like an air conditioning unit.

Sarah breathed a sigh of relief. She leaned out of the helicopter to look down at the ground. It was too high to jump, and the helicopter was gaining altitude quickly.

Rough hands grabbed her from behind and she was yanked around to face a furious Arturo. He shoved the barrel of his gun into her forehead.

Time slowed.

Sarah closed her eyes. At least she would die quickly, like Manuel had.

She'd saved Roman's life. Hopefully he would make it home alive so her death wasn't in vain.

After a moment, Sarah opened her eyes again. Arturo seemed to struggle with himself. His expression smoothed a little and he lowered the gun. He sat down in his seat and pulled her up next to him. His grip wasn't gentle. He kept his hand on her thigh while the helicopter started across the compound.

Her dress had ripped at some point this evening. The fabric split at her ankle and the tear went all the way up to her hip. Arturo's fingers toyed with the material and moved underneath to touch her bare skin.

Sarah stiffened. What was it with Arturo and his men? Was she nothing but an ornament for them to touch?

She'd show *him* what happened when an ornament fought back.

"You have failed," Arturo told her. His lips were a breath away from her ear. It sent a shiver down her spine. He sounded pleased, despite the fact that she'd ruined his assassination attempt. "He will not catch us now. Your assistance will ensure that my plan will come to pass."

"What plan?" Sarah had to shout to be heard.

Arturo held up Ryan's SD card. "This card holds the information I need to mount a terrorist attack on America the likes of which the world has never seen." His hand moved higher on her thigh. "And you'll be there to see it, my dear, right by my side. And afterward, I will take my time killing you. Perhaps I'll bring your Roman to you and make him watch."

Was she hearing him correctly? A terrorist attack on the United States?

That's what Ryan had been doing for him. Not

smuggling drugs... smuggling information.

Sarah felt sick. Roman was right from the beginning. She had no idea what she'd gotten herself into. This was bigger than she was equipped to handle.

If Arturo was able to use the information on that SD card, thousands of people could die.

She was the only one who could stop him.

This was what she'd wanted. A chance to make a difference.

"I won't let you do this."

Arturo's hand stilled on her thigh. He raised an eyebrow. "Do what, my dear?"

"I won't let you use Ryan's information to hurt anyone." Sarah drew herself up to her full height and looked Arturo in the eyes.

He barked a laugh. "You can't stop me, sweetheart."

Sarah eyed the knife handle sticking out of his belt. She smiled her most brilliant smile at him. "Watch me."

She threw herself forward and rammed her head against his nose. At the same time, she used the palm of her hand and whacked his right hand down. The gun he'd been holding clattered to the floor and slid across to the other side of the helicopter.

Arturo reared back with a yell. His other hand tightened painfully on her leg, pinning her in place. He went for the knife in his belt.

Sarah used a forearm to block his attempt to stab her. She wrapped both of her hands around his on the knife handle. The blade shook in the air between them as they each tried to gain control of it.

Arturo stood, towering over her, and used the aid of gravity to bear down on her. The knife's blade inched closer to her chest.

Sarah waited, clenching her teeth.

Just a little longer...

When the blade was just inches from her skin, she lifted her good leg and kicked Arturo as hard as she could in the knee. At the same time, she let go of the knife and rolled to the side and off the seat.

Arturo stumbled forward. The blade went into the fabric cushion and glanced off the metal underneath. He yanked it out and turned, roaring, and dove for her. They both slammed against the back of Tomas's pilot seat.

Arturo grabbed Sarah's hair and pulled, forcing her to the floor. She hit hard, but the helicopter tilted sharply to the left. Arturo landed on top of her and the force of the shift threw him sideways.

Sarah jerked her head up.

Arturo's knife stuck out of Tomas's throat. His head lolled sideways, his hands falling limply from the controls.

The helicopter tilted again, whirling into a deadly spin.

Sarah struggled to her hands and knees, fighting against the centrifugal force that wanted to send her rolling into Arturo's corner. She painstakingly crawled to the other side of the cabin, toward the door. Behind her, she could hear Arturo yelling, but the roar of the engine drowned out his words.

The door handle was so close. Sarah reached out a hand and managed to pull it.

The door slid open.

She strained to see outside. They were somewhere over the middle of the compound.

But it wasn't the ground she needed to worry about.

The tail of the helicopter struck the side of one of the taller adobe buildings. The impact threw Sarah and Arturo into the corner of the cabin like rag dolls. There was a horrible nails-on-chalkboard sound as the propeller screeched into the concrete wall of the building.

Without any momentum to keep them spinning, the helicopter dropped like a rock.

Everything went black.

When she came awake, it was to light and unbearable heat.

She opened her eyes to see bright orange flames licking Tomas's body at the control panel. Arturo lay not too far from her, unmoving. She hoped he was dead, but she didn't have time to check.

Every action movie she'd ever seen told her that she needed to get away, and fast.

Fire in any kind of vehicle was never a good sign.

Sarah moved her fingers and toes, relieved when it seemed she hadn't lost any limbs. Next she systematically moved every body part until she was satisfied that she wasn't seriously injured. Finally, she moved to shift herself into a sitting position and whimpered when blinding pain shot through her midsection.

Oh, God. She could do this.

Gasping, Sarah pushed herself to her hands and knees

and began the painful crawl to the open door. Smoke filled the interior of the helicopter and she coughed, then doubled over in pain.

The SD card. She couldn't leave without it.

Cursing under her breath, Sarah crawled back to Arturo's body. His eyes were closed and it didn't look like he was breathing. She rummaged around in his pockets until she found the small storage device. Her eyes burned and tears streamed down her face. She coughed again and closed her eyes against the pain. She couldn't breathe.

"Sarah!"

She opened her eyes. A dark shadow stood at the helicopter door. "R-Roman?" she rasped.

There was no way he'd be able to hear her.

But somehow, he did.

He dove into the smoke and she saw his face for the first time in what felt like forever. Relief almost made her collapse right there.

"Sarah." Her name sounded like a prayer. "Thank God. Come on, we have to go."

He kneeled next to her and found her hand. His fingers threaded through hers. He tugged her toward the door and she crawled painfully after him.

Roman climbed out and reached back inside. He made as if to pick her up into his arms, but Sarah grabbed his arm and shook her head. "Broken ribs," she explained hoarsely.

He nodded and instead wrapped an arm around her shoulder, supporting her as she limped away from the burning helicopter. Dimly, she could hear shouting in the background. She registered men running everywhere, but she didn't know if they were hers or Arturo's.

They weren't shooting at her, so that was a good sign.

Everyone was too busy running away from the fire.

Once they reached the other side of the street, Roman stopped and turned to her. His eyes swept over her face. "Thank God," he murmured. His hands cradled either side of her head and he looked at her like a man looked at a glass of water in the Sahara. "I didn't think I'd make it in time."

Sarah tried to smile back. "Me neither."

An unintelligible yell sounded behind them, followed by a gunshot. Something pinged off the adobe wall just above their heads. Sarah didn't get a chance to look behind them before Roman tackled her behind a low adobe flowerbed.

She didn't have to look to know it was Arturo. Of course the cockroach was still alive.

Roman swore and covered her with his body. He pulled his gun from his belt and peeked over the top of the wall. Another shot sounded and he quickly ducked back down.

"It's Altez," he told her. He put one hand to his ear. "I've got Sarah. We're pinned down. Altez is taking shots."

Sarah couldn't hear the team's response. Judging from Roman's expression, it wasn't good news. She could hear Arturo yelling at them in Spanish from the other side of the street. His voice sounded closer with each passing second.

They didn't have time to wait for reinforcements.

"Give me your gun."

Roman froze and his gaze flicked down to hers. "What?"

"Your gun. Give me your extra gun!"

The command in her tone must have registered, because he obediently pulled a small handgun from his boot and handed it to her. "What-?"

Sarah flipped off the safety and pushed him off of her. Before he could protest, she rolled out from behind the flowerbed. Her hands weren't as steady as she'd hoped, but she fired a shot at Arturo. It missed, but his face turned into an inhuman snarl and he swung his gun around in her direction.

Roman shot him in the forehead before he could pull the trigger.

Thank God he was a good shot.

Arturo's body crumpled to the street. Not even a second later, the helicopter exploded in a boom that shook the ground beneath them.

Roman dove on top of her again and covered her with his body. Screams echoed all around them, and Sarah heard footsteps as terrified men ran past their fallen leader.

After a few moments, Roman eased off her. "You okay?"

Sarah nodded shakily. She wasn't sure if she was lying.

But she was alive, and for now that was enough.

"Roman!" Emmett and Owen materialized from the smoke. Owen turned his back and watched their surroundings while Emmett kneeled next to Sarah. He gave her a once-over. "Can you walk?"

Sarah glanced down at her ankle and grimaced. It was swollen to triple its size. "I-I think so."

"Okay. Roman will help you. We need to move, now."

Roman took her hand and pulled her to her feet. "It'll be faster if I carry you."

"I don't know which ribs are broken. We'll have bigger problems if I puncture a lung."

Roman nodded grudgingly and gripped her around the shoulders while she wrapped her arm around his waist.

"We've got her. Evac in ten," Emmett said into his earpiece. He raised his gun and signaled to Roman and Sarah. They followed him through the smoke and toward safety.

CHAPTER 20

SARAH AND THE TEAM made it back to the jet without further incident. By the time they reached the airstrip, Sarah was more unconscious than not. Emmett had tried to drive carefully on the bumpy road, but the potholes hadn't been kind to her.

Roman helped her limp onto the plane and settled her in a seat near the door.

The rest of the team was quiet and tense as they made their preparations for departure. Sarah looked out the window as the engines started up and breathed a sigh of relief when the plane finally rose into the air.

Once the danger had passed, the team sprang into action. Roman wrapped a blanket around Sarah's shoulders. She hadn't realized she was shivering, but the warmth was welcome.

Emmett and the others began taking off their gear and stowing it for the flight. Sarah watched the activity through heavy-lidded eyes.

It didn't take long to notice that Dominick favored his

right leg.

"You've been shot," she said in alarm.

Dominick looked down as if he hadn't realized it. "I'll be fine."

"Let me check it out. Roman, grab me a first aid kit. Come sit right here."

Dominick glanced at Emmett as if to get permission. When Emmett nodded, he perched on the chair next to Sarah's and tore a hole in his pants so she could see his wound. It was a clean through-and-through, so Sarah cleaned it and stitched it up.

When she was finished, Dominick nodded his thanks and moved away to chat with Cameron.

Sarah sat still, looking at her dirty, blood-covered hands. Arturo's chilling smile flashed in her mind and she shivered.

He was dead, so why was she still terrified?

"Hey," Emmett said, sitting on the seat next to her.

Sarah looked up, blinking away the moisture in her eyes. "Yeah?"

"I think I was hit with some debris from one of the explosions. I can't tell if there's something still in there. Can you check for me?"

"Yeah." Sarah cleared her throat, thankful for the distraction. "Sure. Of course."

Emmett pulled off his shirt, revealing his bare chest. Sarah bit her lip and forced her expression to remain blank. She hadn't seen his chest since he returned from the hospital last year. A huge scar marred his left side, just under his heart. It was still pink and new-looking, even though it had been healing for almost 18 months.

A chill slid down her spine.

The bullet - or whatever had caused this wound - must have missed his heart by less than an inch.

She could have lost him like she'd lost so many others.

Sarah pulled her gaze away from his scar and focused on the much smaller wound on the back of his shoulder. It was a deep gash, but there wasn't any leftover debris that she could see. Just in case, she flushed it with alcohol and set two small stitches.

Emmett took her hands when she was finished and squeezed one. When Sarah met his eyes, he said, "Glad you're okay."

"Me too." Tears filled her eyes. "Thanks for coming to get me."

Emmett smiled. "Always."

When he moved away, Roman took his place. "You need to rest."

Sarah gave him a once-over, and her gaze stuttered to a stop at the blood staining his side. "You were shot," she exclaimed. Panic made her hands shake.

Ryan's face flashed in her mind.

Not Roman too...

Roman placed a hand on each of her shoulders and met her eyes. "It's just a scratch. I already stitched it up."

Sarah lifted his shirt with one shaking hand and, sure enough, the wound wasn't even bleeding anymore.

"It's in almost the same place as yours," Roman said. "If you can handle it, I think I'll be okay."

Sarah laughed shakily.

"You're in worse shape than all of us combined. Here, let me look at you."

"I'll be fine. Just need to get to a hospital when we get home. There's nothing you can do for me right now."

"But-"

Sarah laid her head on his shoulder, and he quieted. She met Owen's eyes across the aisle and he smiled at her. All of the unspoken regrets and petty arguments between them disintegrated. He apologized with his eyes, and she forgave him. It was how their relationship worked.

Sarah smiled back at her brother and closed her eyes against Roman's shoulder.

She was safe. She was alive.

They had won.

* * * * *

A few days later, Sarah sat in her favorite porch swing on the back deck of her parents' house. She rocked gently back and forth, watching the reflection of the trees swaying in the water of the river.

Her hospital stay had been far too long. If she had any say in the matter, she would've been home after they checked her out. But she had an irate mother and three older brothers to contend with, and they outnumbered her. So she spent an excruciating three days in the hospital under observation.

A broken ankle, two broken ribs, and a third-try stitched up gunshot wound.

She'd definitely seen better days.

Not even fifteen minutes after she got home from the hospital, she was drawn to her spot on the deck. Since her rescue, she couldn't find a moment alone. Someone wanted to be with her every second of every day.

The threat was over now that Arturo was dead, but her family still treated her like she might disappear at any time.

She sighed and looked down at her booted foot. Roman didn't come to see her while she was in the hospital. Emmett said he was back in DC, talking to some bigwigs about Arturo's death and Jeffries' role in the whole thing. The report had to be taken through the proper channels.

Sarah didn't care about that. She wanted to see him. He was supposed to be home this morning.

As if her thoughts had conjured him out of thin air, the screen door opened and Roman stepped out. He looked more relaxed than she'd ever seen him, in casual jeans and a gray t-shirt. His dark hair was cut short and he was freshly-shaven. The scar through his eye was even more prominent than usual.

Sarah looked down at her sweatpants. Her hair hadn't been properly blow-dried in far too long and she hadn't worn makeup since she had dinner with Arturo the week before.

"Hey." Roman sat down on the swing next to her. "Fancy seeing you here."

Sarah eyed him. "Are you following me?"

He smiled. "Just a coincidence. I happened to be passing by. How are you feeling?"

"I can't move around much, but my ribs didn't puncture anything. Only two of them are broken. My ankle is broken in three places -- uh, but I'm fine."

Why was she so nervous?

"Sarah."

She looked up at him. His eyes were warm as he brushed a piece of hair behind her ear. His hand stayed there, caressing her cheek. "I'm glad you're okay."

How did she ever think he was cold? This man was the kindest person she'd ever met.

Sarah closed her eyes and leaned into his hand. "Me too."

"I don't know what I would've done if I lost you."

"Really?"

"Yes." He leaned forward and brushed his lips against hers.

She felt a thrill to her toes. "I missed you too."

Roman chuckled.

Sarah threaded her fingers with his and squeezed tightly. Her thoughts turned to Ryan. Was he smiling down at them from somewhere?

She liked to think he was.

"Roman?"

"Mm?"

"Stay with me."

"Always."

CHAPTER 21

SARAH LIMPED INTO THE ESI OFFICE, cursing her crutches already.

Dominick, who was lounging on the leather couch in the lobby, leaped to his feet. "Do you need help?"

Sarah waved him off with a smile. "Thanks, but I'm good. Where's Emmett?"

"They're waiting for you in his office."

"They?"

Dominick's smile widened and he nodded.

Okay, that was weird.

Sarah limped down the hall and knocked on Emmett's office door. It swung open and she was met with the smiling faces of her brothers. Even Emmett's expression was slightly less severe than usual.

Owen ushered her inside and sat her down.

"W-What's going on?" Sarah asked. "I thought I was coming to take Emmett to lunch."

Chance and Owen moved to stand behind Emmett's chair. Owen's grin was a mile wide.

"I owe you an apology," Emmett said.

"What?"

Her oldest brother stood. He seemed to struggle to find the words. "You wanted to join the team and I turned you down. I thought I wanted to protect you, but I was just underestimating you from the very beginning."

"It's okay, I-"

"Let me finish."

"Okay. Sorry."

Emmett eyed her as if to make sure she wouldn't interrupt again, then continued. "In Mexico, you were the bravest person on the team. You survived what many trained soldiers wouldn't have been able to. Your quick thinking not only saved your life, but the lives of thousands of people. I don't say this often..." He took a deep breath. "But I was wrong."

Owen's grin widened.

Chance struggled to hide a smile.

Sarah's mouth was hanging open. She quickly closed it. "I... don't know what to say. Thank you. That really means a lot."

"I'm not finished." Emmett reached into the top drawer of his desk and pulled out a black SIG Sauer, the same one that all members of the ESI team carried. He set it on the desk in front of her. "You would be a valuable asset to this team. You'll need some field training, but if you still want to join us, we would love to have you."

"I... Really?"

Emmett nodded.

Sarah touched the SIG reverently and picked it up,

weighing it in her palm. It felt... right. More right than anything she'd felt in a long time. "Of course," she whispered, looking up at Emmett. "Of course I want to join the team."

Owen whooped and clapped Emmett on the shoulder. "Just so you know, you're never gonna live this one down. Our grandkids are going to tell stories about the time Emmett Erickson was wrong."

Emmett raised an eyebrow, lips twitching. "And I could tell stories for days about your many shortcomings."

Sarah listened to her brothers' bickering and looked down once more at the SIG in her hand. It was more than a gun; it was a sign that she'd finally found where she belonged.

CHAPTER 22

Six Months Later...

THE SMALL GARDEN behind the chapel was full to bursting on one April day six months later. Everyone in La Conner seemed to be in attendance. The constant barrage of spring rain had disappeared just for today, and dew-speckled flowers gleamed in the early afternoon sun.

Sarah stood in the front row of white wooden chairs that lined either side of the aisle. She craned her head, anxiously scanning the crowd in the garden.

"Relax," Owen said from behind her. His hand gripped her shoulder. "Sit down. There's still time."

Sarah looked at her watch and shot her twin brother an exasperated look. "Two minutes."

Owen grinned and opened his mouth to reply, but he was interrupted.

"Roman has never been late in all the time I've known him," Dominick drawled. He adjusted the cowboy hat on his head and rolled his shoulders.

"You haven't even known him that long," Owen said.

"Doesn't matter. He's reliable."

Sarah smiled, but the nervous flutter in her stomach didn't dissipate. It wasn't until Emmett shot her a quelling look from his seat on Owen's other side that she sat down. She watched Jennifer walk down the aisle and toward the beautiful grand white piano that someone had lent the Ericksons for this occasion.

Sarah wasn't there when they moved the colossal instrument into the garden, but apparently it had given the Erickson brothers - and at least five more men from town - a run for their money.

It was just another example that Bellamy and Chance were deeply loved in La Conner. Their story had spread through the gossip mills over the past six months since Bellamy's return. Everyone read the news reports about her kidnapping, and most people remembered her experiences as a child. She and Chance had become mini-celebrities in town, especially since they'd announced their engagement.

Bellamy's dream of getting married in October had turned out to be a little unrealistic. With everything that happened to Sarah and even Bellamy's own recovery, Chance had stuck his foot down and demanded a spring wedding.

Bellamy had reluctantly agreed.

Sarah was glad they'd waited. It was a perfect day for a wedding, and they'd had plenty of time to plan something really special.

A ceremony that matched the love Bellamy and Chance shared.

Jennifer sat down at the piano and began to play. An expectant hush fell over the crowd and everyone listened as the beautiful melody filled the air in the garden.

Jennifer's belly was as big as a beach ball, and she was only weeks from her due date now. Despite how hard the last few months must have been for her, she looked radiant.

Sarah still felt a rush of guilt every time she saw her, but somehow she knew Jennifer would be fine. And Sarah would spend the rest of her life trying to atone for Tom's death however she could.

As the music began to taper off, Sarah jumped when Roman plopped into the seat beside her. He grinned mischievously in response to her what-the-hell look.

She couldn't even be mad at him when he smiled at her like that.

"Where have you been?"

Roman took her hand and intertwined their fingers.

The music stopped and a wave of awed whispers swept through the crowd.

Sarah craned her neck to see. Chance had materialized at the front of the crowd, looking sharp in his black tuxedo. But that's not what everyone was whispering about.

The door to the chapel had swung open and Bellamy stepped out into the sunlight. She looked like a Disney princess; there was no other way to describe it. Her dark hair, which reached her shoulders now, was curled and hung loosely around her face.

And the dress...

The entire creation was pure white lace. Its heart-shaped bodice hugged her slim waist. A satin belt broke up the continuity and the rest of her dress fell into a full skirt. Lace sleeves reached down to Bellamy's wrists, elegantly covering her scars. She held a small, simple bouquet of red roses in front of her.

But it was the look on her face when she saw Chance down the aisle that melted Sarah's heart. She looked at him as if he was the only person in the world. The happiness on her face was echoed by every pair of eyes that watched her walk down the aisle.

Roman squeezed Sarah's hand. She realized that tears had begun to slip down her cheeks. She laughed and wiped them away so she could watch her brother marry her best friend.

When it came time to exchange vows, an expectant hush fell over the crowd.

Chance took the microphone from the preacher and cleared his throat.

"Bellamy Anne Burke. You are the strongest, most beautiful woman I know and I am damn lucky to have you in my life. It took us too long to stand here today, but I want you to know how deeply I love you. If you'll have me, I will make my arms your shelter, and my heart our home. I vow to keep you safe and to devote myself to you fully. I'll do whatever it takes to make you happy, and we will spend the rest of our lives lost in each other, as husband and wife."

Sarah glanced down the row and saw Emmett wrap his arm around their mother's shoulders. She was smiling as wide as Sarah was, and her eyes were misty.

If only their father could be here to see this.

Sarah's gaze swept back to the couple up front.

Bellamy wiped her eyes and took the microphone from Chance. "It's clear to me now that everything in my life has led me to you. I wouldn't change a single thing, because if I did, I might not be standing here today. Chance Erickson, you are my family. I vow to stand beside you in all things, to weather the storms of life together, and to love you without fear. I give myself to you fully, and I promise to love you until the end of time."

Sarah was smiling so big that her cheeks hurt.

Nothing was more satisfying than this moment.

Bellamy had defied all odds to survive something most people never could. She and Chance had fought through ten years of separation and two murderers to be together.

They were going to be okay.

Sarah looked at her hand in Roman's, and at her family, and the ESI team. This was the only thing she'd ever wanted, even if she didn't know it. Family. A place to belong. People who accepted her as she was and didn't ask her to change.

The minister pronounced Bellamy and Chance husband and wife. A roar of approval went up from the crowd. Chance kissed Bellamy as if it was their first and their last, sweeping her down into a dramatic dip. She came up laughing, her cheeks pink, and they only had eyes for each other.

Sarah stood with everyone else and clapped and waved as the bride and groom made their exit.

No matter what came their way in the future, this was what she needed to remember most.

This was what it meant to be an Erickson.

NEXT IN THE ESI SERIES

Keep reading for a sneak peek at the next book in the ESI series:

LEGACY EXPOSED

Available now!

https://bit.ly/LegacyExposed

CHAPTER 1

There was nothing better than California in the predawn hour.

Abby walked down the deserted neighborhood street. The cool morning breeze played with the ends of her red hair, tossing them across her face as she walked past homes with darkened windows.

It was quiet except for the rhythmic snap of the sole on her left sneaker. Each time she took a step, the sole pulled away from her shoe and slapped back together when she put her weight on it.

This was her last pair of sneakers. Even the duct tape she'd used to hold it together wasn't working anymore. Soon she'd have to dig into her meager savings to buy a new pair.

Abby pushed her hair back over her shoulder, reveling in the feeling of the air on her skin.

Just the morning breeze.

Soon, the sky would turn pink with the sunrise, then blue, and the world would wake up. The streets would fill with locals heading to work and tourists flocking to the beach.

And they'd bring all their noisy emotions with them. Abby's stomach knotted at the thought of it, already preparing for the onslaught she'd face today.

"In, 1, 2, 3, 4…. Out, 1, 2, 3, 4," she muttered, forcing her muscles to relax with each exhale.

Abby checked her watch. 5:15. She had fifteen more minutes to make it to the coffee shop. The morning rush came especially early in the summer when the sun rose earlier and vacationers were out and about, wandering the California beaches with their kids and expensive cameras.

She returned her focus to her breathing and concentrated on the feel of the oxygen rushing into her lungs, then whooshing back out.

She could do this. It was just another normal day for a normal girl.

Yeah, right.

Claire sat on the low brick wall outside of Beach Brews. She looked up and pulled the headphones out of her ears when Abby turned the corner.

"For a second, I thought you called in sick again," she said, smacking her gum. Her pink hair stood straight up like she'd stuck her finger in an electrical socket.

When Abby reached her, a warm glow raced across her skin. It was like she stepped out of the shade and into the sun, except the sun wasn't out yet.

Claire was having a good morning. That was better

than most days.

Abby fumbled in her pocket for the keys and unlocked the door, ignoring the buzzing in the back of her head. "Sorry, I was just running a little late."

"No kidding. Good thing Lonny didn't decide to come in early this morning."

Abby rolled her eyes. "As if he'd have a reason to come in early. He'd rather not come in at all."

Claire snorted. She flounced into the shop and behind the counter while Abby turned on the lights.

It wasn't long before they had the coffee brewing and fresh muffins in the display case. Abby was tying a green apron around her waist when the first customer wandered in.

The buzzing in her head grew a little louder, like the sound of electricity zipping through the power lines above the shop. Abby ignored it.

"Mr. Martinez," she greeted him with a smile. "I have your coffee here. Just a moment."

His eyes crinkled when he smiled. He set a newspaper on the counter and pulled out his wallet. "How are things, Abby?"

"Great, thanks."

What would he say if she answered that question honestly?

Well, Mr. Martinez, I feel like I'm going to throw up and the day has barely started. Also, the bottom of my shoe just fell off.

Abby glanced down, lifting her left foot.

Yep, the sole wasn't attached to her shoe anymore.

With a sigh, she kicked the piece of rubber off to the side and handed Mr. Martinez his cup of coffee, taking his cash in return. "There you go. Have a great day."

He lifted his cup in salute and left the shop.

As the door swung closed, Lonny grabbed it and flung it back open.

The buzzing grew even more intense. Heat crawled across Abby's skin like she'd just opened the oven.

"Good morning, Lonny," she said.

"Is it?" he snapped. "Where's Claire?"

Behind her, Claire popped back into view. "Right here," she sang. She busied herself with sliding a new batch of muffins into the oven, like she'd been working the whole time and not smoking in the employee bathroom.

Lonny grunted. He stomped behind the counter. His large belly barely fit through the opening. "What's that?" he demanded, pointing at the sole of Abby's shoe, which was just peeking out from under the counter.

He didn't miss a thing.

"Nothing," Abby said with a sweet smile. Luckily, it wasn't obvious from above that her left shoe didn't have a bottom.

"Lonny, I need to talk to you about something," Claire piped up. She stepped forward, blocking Lonny's view, and led him toward his office at the back of the store. "I've been thinking about our summer marketing scheme..."

Abby breathed a sigh of relief. The last thing she needed was to be fired today.

The morning rush came quickly after that. Customers filtered in, some cheerful, some impatient, some

— like Lonny - downright ornery.

As usual, the flurry of activity and emotion in the small space hit Abby hard. The buzzing gave her a migraine and the constant temperature shifts made her stomach churn. She ignored all of it, like she always did, and focused on brewing coffee and serving cappuccinos.

During a short lull around ten o'clock, Claire popped another piece of gum in her mouth and leaned on the counter next to Abby.

They watched the crowded beach through the large windows at the front of the store. A family cluttered by, carrying beach towels and boogie boards.

"They look so happy," Claire said longingly. "Must be nice."

Abby didn't have to feel the chill of cold to recognize Claire's sadness. It was in her expression, plain as day. "Is your dad still working a lot?"

"24/7. And Mom's at the gym every night." Claire rolled her eyes. "I might as well not have parents."

Abby's life had taught her about loneliness, and she felt that same emotion in Claire every day.

The only difference was that Claire *had* parents, even if they were never around.

Abby didn't have parents at all.

Claire glanced at her as if reading her mind. "Any luck finding your dad?"

Abby shook her head, straightening the display of chocolates on the counter next to the register. "I'm beginning to think I should just give up. It's like finding a needle in a billion haystacks."

"Aw, don't say that." Claire leaned a hip against the counter. "You can't give up, not until you find him. He's probably looking for you too."

"I doubt it."

Abby's gaze wandered back to the boogie board family. They were currently posing for a photo in front of the beach. The dad was taking the picture, and the mom and kids looked happy as clams.

Bitterness soured her stomach. That kind of life, that kind of family, just wasn't in the cards for her.

The bell above the door chimed as another customer entered the store. Abby cleared her throat and got back to work, grateful that Claire did the same. She didn't want to talk about depressing subjects anymore.

A man stepped up to the counter. A blue baseball cap rested backward on his head. "Mets" was spelled in white and orange lettering on it. He smiled at her as if he recognized her.

"Welcome to Beach Brews," Abby greeted him. "What can I get for you?"

The man extended a hand, jaw popping as his gum switched from one side of his mouth to the other.

What was with people and chewing gum? He and Claire would make a good pair.

"Hi. Are you Abby Simmons?"

Abby frowned. "Um, yes. Can I help you?"

"I'm Robby Adams." He grinned at her. "I know you don't know me, but I've heard about you. Do you have some time? Can I buy you a coffee?"

Was he trying to be charming? Abby didn't have

276

much of a social life, but she wasn't feeling flattered.

More like, creeped out.

"I'm working right now, Mr. Adams, so no, I can't."

"When do you get off?" He offered a charming smile. "I'll wait. I promise it will be worth your time."

Abby hesitated. Before she could tell him no for the second time, the sound of a throat clearing drew her attention.

Claire stood off to the left, in the kitchen and out of Robby's view. She pointed at him, then at Abby, and waggled her eyebrows.

Abby sighed. She should have known.

Claire had made it her personal mission to help Abby "get a life" since they started working together a few months before. She'd already schemed three blind dates that Abby refused.

A romantic relationship was *so* not on her radar. She had more important things to worry about, like finding her father, or a job where she didn't have to interact with a million people every day.

Claire had clearly stepped up her game. If Abby said no to Robby now, her friend would probably come out and force her to talk to him anyway.

"Noon," Abby finally said. "One coffee, that's it."

"Okay, I'll just wait over there. Come find me when you're done." With a cheerful whistle, Robby strolled over to a corner. Abby watched him pull out a laptop and fire it up.

Back in the kitchen, Claire mouthed something that looked like, "Ooh, la la."

Abby stifled a groan. She didn't have time for this. Her migraine was getting worse. She needed to finish her shift and get home before she ended up in a near-comatose state.

Lonny would kill her if she missed any more work.

She served a few more customers and noon approached faster than she wanted it to. She thought about trying to work a bit longer to get some extra cash, but Lonny sent her a scowl when the clock hit 12:05 and she took her cue to clock out.

Claire gave her a light smack on the butt as she passed. Abby glared at her, but she only grinned.

Reluctantly, Abby took a seat across from Robby. He looked up and shot her a flashy smile.

A warm glow spread across her skin. It was enough to make her relax a little and smile back.

"Thanks for agreeing to sit down with me. Claire said you would probably try to escape out the back door."

Abby scowled in the direction of the kitchen. "I'm not *that* rude. I would've told you to get lost before I escaped out the back door."

Robby laughed. "I'm glad I caught you on a good day then."

The pounding in her head reminded her that it was not a good day, but Abby didn't contradict him. Even though he showed up unannounced, he seemed nice.

And he had a great smile.

"Tell me about yourself, Robby Adams," she said.

"The short version or the long version?" Robby closed his laptop and sat back.

"You've got about fifteen minutes to wow me."

"Come on, Abby," Claire said, stepping up to their table with two steaming cups of coffee. "Give the poor guy a break. You've got more than fifteen minutes."

Abby shot her a look. "I have a lot to do today. Errands to run, and – "

"Don't let her run out early," Claire said, ignoring Abby. "She doesn't have a social life, so she has no other plans today."

Abby's jaw dropped.

Robby laughed. "Thanks for the tip, but I was hoping that my charm would keep her around."

"Good luck with that." Claire winked and returned to her place behind the counter.

Abby took a sip of her coffee, praying that the steam would hide her burning cheeks. Claire would pay for that later; Abby would have to think about a suitable punishment.

"What's got you so busy after work?" Robby asked, one eyebrow raised. "Since, apparently, you have no social life."

Abby groaned. "Claire has a big mouth."

Robby slid his laptop off the table and looked at her expectantly.

Her mind went blank. She couldn't come up with a single lie that he might believe.

"I... have this project that I'm working on," she said slowly. "I'm trying to find my birth father."

Robby tilted his head. "You're adopted?"

"Not exactly." Abby warmed her fingers on the

outside of the coffee cup. "My mom died when I was a baby."

"Oh, I'm sorry to hear that. And your dad wasn't in the picture?"

"No." Abby looked down. She didn't know why she was telling him any of this. Maybe it was the warm feeling he gave her, or the fact that she'd just hit another dead end in her search. "I have no idea who he is. I've spent the last few years trying to find him, but I haven't had any luck."

"Hmm, interesting." Robby glanced toward the counter, where Claire was chatting with a customer. "Did Claire tell you what I do for a living?"

Abby frowned. "No. She didn't tell me anything about you."

"I'm a reporter for the Ventura County Star."

She groaned. "Of course you are. She thought you could help me."

Robby smiled. "I do puff pieces, mostly, but I do have some connections. And, what do you know, I'm between projects right now."

"I can't ask you to do that."

"You didn't. I offered." Robby moved his coffee cup to her side of the table and pulled his laptop from the bag at his feet. "If you tell me what you know about him, I'll see what I can find. We'll call it a favor for a friend."

Abby glanced at Claire. The little schemer met her eyes over the shoulder of the customer at the counter and grinned. Then she looked back at Robby, who waited expectantly, hands hovering over his keyboard.

"All right," she conceded. "But it's not much. I know

I was born in Denver. I tried to figure out which hospital, but none of them would release the records to me. My mom's name was Natalie Simmons. When I was six months old, we were in a car accident. Our car rolled and ended upside down in a creek."

Robby's fingers, flying across the keys, stopped. He glanced up at her. "Upside down in a creek?"

Abby nodded. "There's a news article about it. It happened somewhere in Washington. They said it was a DUI. Drugs, I think. My mom drowned, but my car seat was just out of the water. Rescuers were able to get me out."

"That's... amazing. I mean, it's tragic, but what a story."

"Yeah, quite the story. I don't remember it, obviously. But I hired a private investigator to look into it last year, hoping he could find some link to my father or a reason that my mom would've been in another state, on drugs, with a baby in the backseat."

Robby reached across the table.

Abby froze. Was he reaching for her hand? Touching people made the buzzing in her head unbearable, but it would be rude to yank her hands off the table.

She opened her mouth to protest, but Robby's hand slid past hers and wrapped around his coffee cup. He pulled it back and took a sip.

Abby released a breath.

"I'll look into this," Robby said. He scribbled something on a piece of paper that he pulled from the computer bag at his feet. "Here's my email address. Send me all your information and I'll see what I can find."

"Thanks," Abby said, sliding it into her pocket. "I will."

Robby closed his laptop. "So what happened to you after that? Where did you go?"

"Foster care."

He whistled. "That's rough."

"I wouldn't recommend it, that's for sure."

That was an understatement. After years of loneliness and more homes than she could count, Abby graduated high school early and struck out on her own.

She'd thought that getting her own apartment, a place she could call home, would make her life better.

Instead, she'd found a different kind of loneliness.

Shortly after that, she started searching for the only missing piece that could make the puzzle of her past fit together.

Her father.

Not that it did her any good. Five years later, she still hadn't found him.

Robby stood up. "I'll do everything I can to help." "With any luck, my connections will find something useful. They haven't failed me yet."

Abby smiled. "Thanks, Robby. I appreciate it."

After they exchanged phone numbers and said their goodbyes, she watched him saunter out of the coffee shop.

For the first time in years, she felt something warm in her chest, something entirely her own.

Hope.

THANKS FOR READING!

Thank you so much for supporting me and my work. Please consider leaving an honest review on either Amazon or GoodReads. They are so important to authors, and I'd love to know what you think! Don't forget to share your review on social media with the hashtag *#counterplay* and recommend this book to your friends!

DON'T FORGET TO SIGN UP FOR MY MONTHLY NEWSLETTER

TO RECEIVE SPECIAL OFFERS, GIVEAWAYS, DISCOUNTS, BONUS CONTENT, UPDATES FROM THE AUTHOR, INFO ON NEW RELEASES AND OTHER GREAT READS:

WWW.CEARANOBLES.COM/SUBSCRIBE

ACKNOWLEDGMENTS

It takes an army to take a story from a brief glimpse of an idea to the fully-realized book sitting in your hands.

I'm so blessed that I've got the best army behind me!

Thank you so much to my husband, Grady, for always supporting me and pushing me to be my best. And for volunteering to take the baby so Mama can get some work done. I love you forever!

I'm so thankful to my sweet mother-in-law, Jolyn, who took the baby for a week so I could mad-dash to finish this book by my deadline.

And to my beta readers – Shae, Beth, Jolyn (thanks twice!), and my adorable mom, Alicia.

My cover designer, Les, took a tiny idea and turned it into the beautiful cover on the front of this book. Thank you!

And most importantly, to you, dear reader. Without you, this book wouldn't be here. I'm continually humbled by your reviews, and for trusting me as your next book purchase. I owe you everything!

Ceara Nobles is a Utah-based author of romantic suspense and fantasy novels. She graduated from the University of Utah in 2016 with a B.A. in Computer Animation, then realized she hated it. So she decided to pursue her true love of writing instead. She spends her days writing sales copy as a copywriter... and her evenings writing exciting stories as an author. And she loves both! When she's not busy writing, you can find her snuggling her new baby girl, road tripping with her hubby, or shooing her cats off her laptop.

CONNECT WITH CEARA ON:

Website: www.cearanobles.com
Facebook: @cearanoblesauthor
Instagram: @cearanoblesbooks
Twitter: @cearanobles
GoodReads: Ceara Nobles

Made in United States
North Haven, CT
05 October 2022